'Look…Xavier…we hardly know each other. I'm not normally—'

'So responsive? Well, neither am I.' His voice sounded harsh.

She had been about to say *easy*, but amended her words. 'That is…I mean…I want you to know that it wasn't my intention to come here just for some kind of holiday…thing.'

He moved her closer to him, looping deceptively loose arms around her waist, ignoring the chatter around them, and she came in contact with the still semi-hard evidence of his arousal. Immediately an answering liquid heat pooled in her groin.

'And, contrary to what you may think, I'm not in the habit of pursuing random tourists… I'm not sure what this is either, but don't you think it might be fun to explore?'

Fun. Explore. The words resounded in her head.

Abby Green worked for twelve years in the film industry. The glamour of four a.m. starts, dealing with precious egos, the mucky fields, driving rain...all became too much. After stumbling across a guide to writing romance, she took it as a sign and saw her way out, capitalising on her long-time love for romance books. Now she is very happy to sit in her nice warm house while others are out in the rain and muck! She lives and works in Dublin.

CHOSEN AS THE FRENCHMAN'S BRIDE

BY
ABBY GREEN

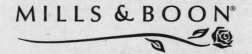

All the characters in this book have no existence outside the imagination of the author, and have no relation whatsoever to anyone bearing the same name or names. They are not even distantly inspired by any individual known or unknown to the author, and all the incidents are pure invention.

First published in Great Britain 2006
Paperback Edition 2007
Harlequin Mills & Boon Limited,
Eton House, 18-24 Paradise Road, Richmond, Surrey TW9 1SR

© Abby Green 2006

ISBN-13: 978 0 263 85290 5
ISNB-10:   0 263 85290 3

Set in Times Roman 10½ on 11¼ pt
01-0107-57107

Printed and bound in Spain
by Litografia Rosés, S.A., Barcelona

CHOSEN AS THE FRENCHMAN'S BRIDE

For Lynn and the women upstairs...

PROLOGUE

The poolside, Hotel Lézille, 8.30pm

HE NOTICED her as soon as she appeared in the archway between the lobby and the pool, his eyes drawn there as if pulled by a magnetic force. A rare excitement stirred his pulse. He told himself that he hadn't come especially to seek her out. She seemed slightly hesitant, unsure. She wasn't the most beautiful woman he'd ever seen, but she had a stunningly natural quality about her, which in his world was rare, compelling. In a simple black dress that outlined every slender curve and a generous bosom, she caught his eye *again*, and he couldn't look away. Didn't want to.

The soft waves of her dark hair framed her face. Intriguingly, she seemed to be slightly self-conscious. Or perhaps, he thought with a hardened cynicism that had been honed over years, she carefully projected that vulnerable fragility. God knew she had managed to capture his attention in the street yesterday. Her huge, striking blue eyes had momentarily stunned him, rendering him speechless. And he was never stunned, or speechless. Something in their depths had caught him, combined with that lush mouth, looking up at him so innocently, full of a shocked kind of awe.

Then, amazingly, when he had seen her on the island earlier today, he had followed some base instinct to see her up close again… She was everything he remembered, and more. He recalled how she had trembled under his hands in the street yesterday, and under his look earlier today on the island. He couldn't ever remember a woman being so blatantly responsive.

His mouth compressed when he thought of her refusal to have dinner with him. That certainly hadn't happened in a while, if ever. Was she playing some game? He wouldn't be surprised… He was constantly amazed at the lengths some women went to just to get his attention. Playing hard to get wasn't a new trick…

He mentally dismissed the bottle redhead to his left, who was chattering incessantly, oblivious of the fact that his attention had long wandered from her far too obviously surgically enhanced assets.

With a barely perceptible flick of his wrist a man materialised at his side, bending low.

'Yes, sir?'

'Who is that woman?' He indicated to where she stood.

'She's not a guest with us, sir, but I can find out if you like…'

He just shook his head and dismissed him.

The ennui that had settled over him recently was definitely fading as he took in her graceful progress through the tables to reach her companions. With a skill based on years of reading people and body language, a skill that had tripled his fortune many times over, he assessed them in seconds, focusing on the man he guessed was her date. No competition. His heart-rate speeded up pleasantly as he contemplated them from under hooded lids. He decided now that he would conveniently forget the blow to his pride when she had refused him earlier. She was definitely worth pursuing. A surge of anticipation and desire made him feel alive in a way he hadn't in months…

CHAPTER ONE

Earlier that day...

JANE VAUGHAN wandered up and down the bustling jetty with a frown appearing over the ridge of her sunglasses. She couldn't remember exactly which gate she'd been at yesterday; now there were lots of bobbing boats and people lining up to get on board. The man she'd approached had taken no deposit, nor given her a ticket, but instead had reassured her that if she came back to him he would make sure she got on the right boat...the only problem now was that she couldn't spot him anywhere.

Bumping into that stranger in the street just afterwards must have scrambled her brain more than she'd thought. She shook her head wryly. She'd never thought herself to be the kind of woman that would spend a night fantasising about someone she had bumped into for mere moments. A newly familiar heat flooded her belly, however, as his tall, powerful body and hard-boned face swam into her mind's eye, his image still as vivid as if he were standing right in front of her. She shook her head again, this time to shake free of the memory. Honestly, this was so unlike her.

She went towards a gate that looked familiar, tagging onto the end of a queue. When she got to the man at the top he seemed a little harassed. At her query of, *'Excusez-moi. C'est le bâteau pour les îles?'* he just gestured impatiently into the boat. She hesitated for a moment, before figuring what was the worst that could happen? So if she didn't end up exactly where she'd expected to then it would be an adventure. They were going somewhere, and she was on holiday, not everything had to be strictly organised. She needed to relax more.

Once they were underway she had to admit grudgingly that she was enjoying the breeze and the sun across her shoulders and bare legs. The brightly patterned halterneck dress she wore was a present from her friend Lisa, given with an order to make herself more visible.

She pushed her sunglasses onto her head, tipping her face up to the sun, and for the first time since landing on the Côte D'Azur a week ago felt a rush of wellbeing and freedom. She didn't even really miss her friend's presence. Lisa was meant to have travelled with her—after all, it was *her* family's villa that Jane was staying in. But at the last minute Lisa's father had been rushed into hospital with a suspected heart attack, and this very week was undergoing a delicate operation. The conversation she'd had with Lisa the night before her departure had been rushed, but her friend had been insistent.

'Janey, if you don't go then I'll feel guilty on top of everything else. Anyway, you'll be doing us a favour. No one has been at the house for months, and it needs to be aired, so look at it like that.'

'But I can't just leave when you might need me most…'

'Look,' Lisa pointed out, 'you know my family. It'll be like Picadilly Circus in the hospital, and we've been assured Dad is going to be fine… Seeing your little face here would only upset me, and I mean that in a good way.'

She knew Lisa was just being brave, that the outcome was anything but assured, and didn't want to put her under any more pressure.

'OK, OK.'

Jane had given in. Lisa was right; there wasn't anything she could do. With a formidable mother, four sisters and three brothers she would only get in the way. And of the three brothers one in particular was intent on pursuing Jane. Not sure how she felt about Dominic, who was lovely, if a little dull, Jane was well aware that the campaign would have been taken up with enthusiasm by Lisa had she had the opportunity.

She got up and wandered over to the railing, shades back on against the glare of the sun, the sea spray catching her every now and then.

She still couldn't help a little pang of guilt at enjoying her solitude so much. She really hadn't expected to embrace it, but for the first time in her twenty-six years she was truly alone, without the crushing responsibility she'd carried for so long. And it felt good!

Looking up from her contemplation of the foaming sea, she saw that they were approaching an island. Something about it, rising majestically from the water, made her shiver—as if someone had just run a finger down her spine. It was a forbidding rock, softened only by the sandy beach and picturesque houses that surrounded the small harbour. The sun glinted off the water as the boat docked and they disembarked. On the jetty, as she waited with the other passengers to be told where to go, her mind wandered back to danger territory, as if it had been waiting patiently in the wings until she'd stopped thinking of other things. She tried to resist, but it was too strong, yet again she re-lived the events of yesterday...that burning moment in the streets near the harbour came flooding back.

She'd escaped the crowded pedestrian area, feeling somewhat claustrophobic, and stumbled into a charming winding street that had been blessedly quiet, with no sign of any tourists. She had looked for a street name to figure out where she was; she wanted to explore more of this sleepy part of the town.

With her map open, trying to walk and read at the same

time, she'd been unaware of the approaching corner. She had looked up briefly, there had been a flash of something, and she'd crashed into a wall.

Except it hadn't been a wall, because a wall wouldn't have reached out and clamped hard hands on her upper arms. Winded and stunned, the map slipping from her fingers, she'd realised that she'd bumped into a man. Her gaze, on a level with a T-shirt-clad broad chest, had moved up, and up again, before coming face to face with the most beautiful pair of green eyes she'd ever seen—like the green of a distant oasis in the desert—in a dark olive-skinned face, with black brows drawn together forbiddingly. Her jaw had dropped.

It had been only then that she'd become aware of her own hands, curled around his biceps, where they had gone automatically to steady herself. And with that awareness had come the feel of bunched muscle beneath his warm, silky skin. They had flexed lightly under her fingertips as his arms held her, and out of nowhere came a spiking of pleasure so intense and alien through her entire body that she'd felt her eyes open wide in shock. His gaze had moved down to her mouth, and she'd had a weightless, almost out-of-body feeling, as if they hadn't been in a side street, as if this hadn't really been happening.

The spell had been jarringly broken when a shrill voice had sounded. Jane's gaze had shifted with effort to take in a stunning blonde woman rounding the corner, her stream of incomprehensible French directed at the man. His hands had tightened momentarily before he'd dipped from view and come back up with her map in his hand. He'd held it out to her wordlessly, a slightly mocking smile on his mouth. She'd taken it, and before she had even been able to say sorry, or thank you, the blonde had grabbed the man's attention and with a scant glance at Jane had urged him away, looking at her watch with exaggerated motions. And he had disappeared.

Jane had stood, still stunned, her body energised to a

point of awareness just short of pain. She had still been able to feel the imprint of his hands on her arms. She'd lifted fingers to her lips, which had tingled…as if he had actually touched them. It had been just seconds, a mere moment, but she'd felt as though she'd stood there with him for hours. The most bizarre and disturbing feeling. And then she had remembered his enigmatic smile, as if he'd known exactly what effect he was having on her. Arrogant, as if it was expected.

Jane's reverie ended abruptly as she found that she was following the other tourists onto a small air-conditioned bus. She vowed that that was the last time she would indulge herself in thinking about that man. The last time she would indulge the fantasy she'd had of sitting across a table from him, sharing an intimate dinner, candlelight flickering, picking up the silverware and sparkling glasses. Those green eyes holding hers, not letting her look away. She quashed the silly flutter in her belly and took in the other people on the bus, leaning over to a young couple about her age across the aisle.

'Excuse me, do you know where we are?'

The woman leant across her boyfriend, replying with a strong American accent. 'Honey, this is Lézille Island—but you'd know that, coming from the hotel…aren't you a guest?

'No!' Jane clapped a hand to her mouth. 'I'm not in a hotel…I thought this was just a general trip…'

Dismayed, she wondered what she should do, she hadn't paid for this trip… She belatedly remembered asking the man if this was the boat to *les îles*—the islands, in French, which sounded exactly like the name of this island. Lézille. No wonder he had just ushered her on board.

The other woman waved a hand. 'Oh, don't worry. I won't say anything, and no one will notice…you just bagged yourself a free trip!'

Jane smiled weakly. She hated any sort of subterfuge. But maybe it wasn't such a big deal. She could always follow them back to their hotel afterwards and offer to pay for the trip. She felt a little better with that thought.

The woman told her that they were due to visit a vineyard for some wine-tasting, and afterwards to take in an aerial display. Jane gave in and relaxed, and started to enjoy the mystery tour nature of the trip…this was exactly what she needed.

The vineyard was enormous, with beautifully kept rows of vines. They were shown every part of the winemaking process—which Jane had to admit was more interesting than she would have expected. The name on the bottles sounded familiar—as had the name of the island.

When they emerged at the other end of the buildings, they could see what looked like a medieval castle in the distance. Again she felt that funny sensation…almost like déjà vu.

'You know this island is owned by a billionaire who lives in that castle?'

Jane looked around the see the friendly woman from the bus. 'No…no, I don't know anything about it.'

Her voice lowered dramatically. 'Well, apparently he owns half the coast too—his family go back centuries… He's so private, he only allows people to visit a few times a year. There's all sorts of stories about—' She broke off when her boyfriend came and dragged her away to see something.

Jane looked back to the castle. It certainly looked as if it could have been around in the Middle Ages. On a small island like this, she guessed it could have been some kind of protective fortress.

After another short trip in the bus, along a picturesque strip of coastline, they were deposited in a big green field, full of wild flowers, with an airstrip at the far end. A dozen planes were lined up in readiness. There was a fiesta-like atmosphere, with families stretched out around the ground with picnics, stalls set up with drinks, food and handicrafts. A small stone building to the side looked like some kind of museum, and on closer inspection Jane discovered that it was. She just gave it a brief look, before wandering over to see the stalls, where she bought some bread and cheese for a light lunch, noticing that everyone else seemed to have brought picnics.

Suddenly her arm was grabbed. 'We haven't introduced ourselves. I'm Sherry, and this is Brad. We're on honeymoon from New York. You should stick with us if you're on your own.'

The woman from the bus barely allowed Jane to get a word in edgeways to introduce herself as they led her away to a spot they had picked out on the grass. It was nice to have the company as she ate her meagre lunch, and they turned out to be very friendly, insisting on sharing their wine and fruit.

After lunch Jane noticed men in flight suits walking towards the small planes from a hangar area, and the crowd got up and started to cheer. Soon there was one last pilot walking to his plane. With the sun in her eyes, he just was a shape in the distance.

A hush went around the field and, wondering at the strange reaction, Jane lifted a hand to shade her eyes—and stiffened when she saw more clearly who it was. It was the man from the street; she was sure of it. He was unmistakable. His impressive build and height set him apart.

Before she knew what she was doing she was on her feet with the rest of the crowd. He had an innately powerful grace, commanding attention as he strode towards the plane. Clearly the leader. On a gesture from him, the other pilots started up.

When he got into the plane, something in Jane's stomach fell, and she found she couldn't sit down again and relax. As they took off one by one, he being the last, she unconsciously clenched her fists. The display probably only took fifteen minutes but to Jane it seemed to go on for ever. Her eyes never left his plane, a ball lodging in her gut. She couldn't explain or fathom the completely irrational fear she felt; she just knew that nothing could move her from the spot until that plane was back on the ground and he walked out, safe.

He flew as though he had a death wish. Dizzying turns and ever increasingly daring stunts had the crowd gasping in unison and clapping. He was the last to land, watched by the other pilots, their respect obvious.

When he stepped out of the plane to thunderous applause, Jane unclenched her fists, noticing that her nails had carved half moons into her palms. Unbelievably she felt anger towards him—this complete stranger!

The sun must be getting to her, she thought, unable to tear her eyes away. As the crowd surged towards the planes, his head turned, and even though at least fifty metres separated them, his gaze caught hers. She had a freefall feeling, couldn't move. She felt as if he had reached out and touched her with those amazing eyes. With a supremely difficult struggle she turned away, and almost fell to the ground beside the American couple, who were chattering happily, oblivious to her inner turmoil. Maybe she *had* actually become delusional…conjured him up out of her rampant imagination.

When Brad and Sherry got up to check out the small museum she followed gratefully, feeling inexplicably as if she was escaping something…

She cast a quick glance back towards the planes, unable to help herself. She could just see the top of his dark head, surrounded by people—mainly adoring women from the looks of it.

She turned away resolutely and ducked inside, reassuring herself that by the time they came out all the pilots would be gone. After a few minutes she was feeling somewhat calmer, and walked around taking in the information with genuine interest. From a small plaque that was tucked into a corner she learned about a devastating earthquake at the turn of the century, which had reduced the population of nearly a thousand to a few hundred. It was only in recent decades that the island had begun to thrive again.

Apparently it had been in the hands of one family since

the time of the crusades. They were called Salgado-Lézille, and had come originally from Spain. That would explain the hacienda-like houses Jane thought, remembering seeing them dotted around the harbour and elsewhere. And in retrospect there was something vaguely Moorish about the shape of the majestic castle.

She had turned to follow the crush out the door when the light was blocked momentarily and someone came in.

It was him. Even before she saw his face she knew. He scanned the room as people passed by him, and Jane held her breath. Slowly his gaze came to rest on her and stopped. Immediately her heart started to thump and her legs turned to jelly.

He stared at her.

Jane shook herself mentally. This was crazy. How could she be reacting like this *again*? She turned away and looked back at a document behind the glass, but she could see his shape reflected. He wasn't moving. She forced herself to walk around the exhibit again and admonished herself. She was going to have to leave sooner or later, and there was no way he would have come in just to stare at her.

But he was. She could feel it.

All she had to do was walk past him. Easy.

She followed the chattering line of other tourists heading out, drawing ever closer to the door, looking anywhere but at the disturbing man and his large, broad-shouldered body leaning insouciantly against the wall. She sensed his dark gaze, hot and heavy upon her, like a physical caress, and trembled.

Now there were only two people in front of her. Why had they stopped? She dampened down her irritation. Her reaction was completely over the top. She just needed to get back out into the fresh air. That must be it, she comforted herself—the heat. As if to prove her point, she felt a trickle of sweat between her breasts.

She could see his long legs crossed at the ankles. She focused on the back of the heavy loud man in front of her. Maybe she could pretend she was with him, ensuring a smooth passage past. She had no idea why it was so important; she just felt it deep in the core of her being.

She was almost beside him now, the breath hitching in her throat. He took up her peripheral vision. She didn't have to be looking at him to know what he was like. Despite only the brief moment the day before, and her distant view earlier today, she knew she would be able to describe him in detail.

Thick dark hair, swept high off a strong broad forehead. Harsh, vitally masculine face, lines broken only by an aquiline nose, sensually sculpted lips. And those mesmerising eyes, the eyelashes visible even from a distance. His flight suit enhanced his commanding physique.

'Oh, my God, he is gorgeous.'

You don't say, Jane thought wryly at Sherry's indiscreetly loud whisper behind her. Without looking she could feel his sardonic smile. He had heard and understood; he must speak English.

She was almost at the door, almost home free, when her wrist was captured in an electrifying grip by a familiarly strong lean hand. The people behind her jostled, and to avoid a crush she had to move closer, go with the pull of the hand. Her blue eyes huge, she looked up at him.

He drew her in, close to his body, the people pushing past her inadvertently moving her in even closer. She could feel the heat of his thigh, hard against her own through the thin material of her dress.

What was happening?

She looked up, the question on her face, captivated by his gaze, which looked back down at her, lazily assessing. This man who had dominated nearly her every thought since yesterday.

'What are you looking at?' she croaked.

'You,' he answered with deceptive simplicity, and the word rocked through Jane's body.

'Who…who are you?'

He didn't answer, just kept a loose, yet immovable grip on her wrist. She could feel her pulse thumping against the warm skin of his hand like a captured bird. Something in her blood leapt, and excited anticipation built in her belly. The part of her that he had reached yesterday, unknown and alien, was coming to life again…just under his look. He smiled indolently, before his eyes left hers to look her up and down so thoroughly that she felt naked, exposed. A flush spread from her belly all the way up to her neck. She tried to yank her wrist away to no avail; his grip only tightened. He couldn't possibly remember her, could he?

Nerves made her blurt out, 'Who do you think you are? How dare you look at me like that…?'

His eyes bored into hers, the green becoming darker, making him look dangerous, 'You pretend to not recognise me?'

He remembered.

'No…well, that is, yes. I saw you yesterday in the street… when you bumped into me.'

'As I recall it was the other way around, *n'est ce pas*?'

His voice sounded as though it had been dipped in honey treacle, deep and dark, with only the barest hint of an accent, his English flawless. She was finding it hard to concentrate.

'I was just reading a map. Surely you saw me…' She cursed the breathless tone in her voice.

He ran a quick glance up and down again. 'Oh, I saw you all right.'

She saw the amusement lurking in his eyes and she tried to pull away again. This time he let her go, and she felt inexplicably bereft.

'You should have been looking where you were going. You could have collided with a more…immovable object.'

From what she could remember, all too well, *he* had been

like a wall…a wall of hard-packed muscle. She felt her legs weaken. More than disturbed by the effect he was having on her, she looked at him incensed,

'The street was empty…it's hardly a crime to divert one's attention for a moment.'

He inclined his head in a surprisingly old-fashioned gesture. 'Maybe we can agree that we were equally to blame.'

She huffed slightly. 'It's no big deal.'

'Yet you are the one who seems to be upset about it,' he pointed out, picking up on her discomfort.

Jane looked around then, and saw that they were alone in the building. Everyone else had disappeared. When had that happened?

She looked out through the door and sighed with relief when she saw the bus, where the others were embarking. She turned to find him right behind her, and stepped back hurriedly.

'I have to go…that's my bus leaving now.'

He caught her hand just as she turned away. Her pulse leapt again.

'Would you do me the honour of being my dinner guest tonight? To…foster a truce and allow me to make amends for my part in our collision.'

He was smooth, and practised, and too, too seductive. Jane shook her head, slightly dazed. He was asking her out for dinner? Her eyes met his. *No way, no way*, went through her mind. This man was so out of her league that he might as well be from another planet. She didn't have the wherewithal to sit across a table from him! She'd dissolve in a puddle within minutes. And the way he was looking at her…as though he wanted to have *her* for dinner!

'I'm sorry,' she said stiffly, pulling her hand free. 'I…I have arrangements made already, but thank you for asking.'

His eyes probed hers for an uncomfortably long moment, and then he shrugged lightly, a shuttered look descending over his face. 'Very well.'

Now she had offended him, she thought miserably. Without knowing what to say or do, she stepped away and half ran, half walked back to the bus.

She sank into her seat breathing heavily. She felt hot and bothered, her hand still tingling where he had caught it. Jane evaded Sherry's very pointed look and stared out of the window.

All the way back to the mainland she veered between feeling as if she had made a lucky escape and extreme self-recrimination. Since bumping into him she had thought of little else, even fantasised about having dinner with him, but when she was offered the opportunity what did she do? Refused point-blank.

She didn't deserve a date with such a man if she couldn't even handle being asked out. And *why* had he asked her out? She couldn't fathom it. She could tell that he was mannerly—perhaps it was a pilot thing, a code of conduct? Although somehow he didn't look like just a pilot. Her brain began to throb. She couldn't help but feel as though she had let herself down in some way. She could well imagine Lisa's reaction.

Back on land, she sighed to herself, trying to catch a glimpse of the island which was too far away to view in the late-afternoon haze. She would just have to put it down to experience. A man like Lisa's brother Dominic was obviously all she could handle…maybe this was a sign.

When she saw the others get on the bus for their hotel she followed them on board.

Fifteen minutes later they pulled off the road and into a resort. It screamed extreme wealth. Immaculate lawns and manicured gardens led up to a beautiful hacienda-style building, all in white. In the early dusk lights shone from the windows, gauzy curtains fluttering in the breeze. She read the name of the hotel carved discreetly into a low stone wall, and only registered then how well dressed her companions were.

She had tagged on to a day trip from one of the Lézille Hotels. No wonder the name had sounded familiar. The owner of the island obviously also owned this very well-known string of resorts dotted all over the world in prime locations and renowned for their discretion, luxuriousness, exclusivity.

She followed the others into the lobby and they split off in different directions. Just as she went to look for the tourist office Sherry stopped her. 'Hey, Jane, why don't you come back here for dinner tonight? You said you were on your own, and we've made friends with a guy from Washington DC who works in town... We could make a foursome; he'd love your accent.'

Jane opened her mouth on reflex to say no, and stopped herself. Had she learnt nothing from her recent experience? Here she was, being offered another chance. She smiled at Sherry. 'I'd love to.'

'Plus, I want to hear all about your conversation with Mr Gorgeous!'

Jane's smile faded. They would most certainly *not* be discussing that. She made a mental note to make sure the conversation never strayed into that area.

Once she had sorted out payment for the trip with a very bemused tour manager she made her way back to the villa.

A few hours later Jane was in a taxi on her way back to the hotel. She hoped that her mystery date was tall. She was five foot nine herself in flats, and if he wasn't they would look ridiculous. Unlike *him*—she knew she could wear the highest heels and would still have to look up. Her heart started to thump, just thinking of what it would be like to be on the way to meet *him*... *But you were a chicken and turned him down.* As if she needed to be reminded...

The taxi pulled into the front courtyard and Jane made a last-ditch effort to erase his image. She made her way out to the poolside buffet, where she had arranged to meet the others, and Sherry's madly waving arm caught her attention easily enough—along with the sparkly half-dress she was wearing. She weaved through the tables to get to them, completely oblivious of several admiring glances on the way. And one in particular from the other side of the pool.

CHAPTER TWO

'JANE! Meet Pete—he split up with his fiancée back home a few months ago and moved here to lick his wounds.'

Jane had to hold back a smile at Sherry's effervescent indiscretion, and stuck out her hand to the other man. 'Pleased to meet you. I'm Jane Vaughan.'

He was pleasantly attractive, with nothing overpowering about him—brown hair, brown eyes, nice smile. No chemistry whatsoever. Jane relaxed, and they settled into a light easy conversation. When the band struck up a slow jazzy tune Pete stood and asked her to dance. As she went into his arms on the dance floor she had to admit that it was all very agreeable. This was much more her scene than the messily overwhelming attraction she had felt for the stranger. Heat induced lust. This she could handle. That… She shivered at the thought.

Pete tightened his arms around her. 'Hey, are you cold?'

Jane immediately recoiled, surprised at the strength of her reaction. 'No!' she said, far too quickly, amending it with a smile. 'No…just a little tired. Maybe if we could sit down again…'

As they approached the table another woman was leaving and waving gaily at Sherry, who turned gleaming eyes on Jane as she sat down. 'You'll never guess what I just found out.'

Jane obediently supplied, 'What?'

The men took themselves off to the bar, muttering something about women and gossip. It made Jane cringe a little, but Sherry was leaning over the table, saying with a loud whisper, 'That guy…the gorgeous hunk from earlier…well, don't look now, but he's behind you on the other side of the pool, and he's been looking this way.'

Immediately Jane's back straightened, and she started breathing faster. She just managed to stop herself from turning around, but Sherry was doing it for her, looking over Jane's shoulder. A frown marred her pretty features,

'Shoot—he's gone. Oh, well…anyway, wait till you hear what I found out from Tilly Brown. He's Mr Island!' She looked at Jane as if to say, *Don't you get it?* Jane just looked back blankly. What on earth did she mean?

Sherry sighed exaggeratedly. 'He owns the island we were on today. *He's* the billionaire. His name is—get this for a mouthful—Xavier Salgado-Lézille, and he owns this whole complex too. Can you believe that? To think that we saw him and didn't know. I'm so dumb…'

Jane sat there stunned as Sherry chattered on. It made sense now—his presence, the authority he commanded. She recognised that he must have assumed she was a guest at the hotel. His reaction to her refusal earlier didn't surprise her now. She doubted that many women would turn down someone like him.

'And the best thing is,' Sherry continued, pausing for dramatic effect, 'he's a bachelor. Well, actually a notorious playboy, incapable of commitment some say—they call him the Prince of Darkness because he's so dark and brooding and—'

'You really shouldn't listen to idle gossip you know.'

The deep voice beside them could have cut through steel. They both looked up to find the object of their conversation beside the table. The epitome of wealth and sophistication in an impeccable tuxedo. The man who had loomed large in

Jane's imagination for two days now had a name—and an island, a hotel chain, a wine label, a reputation. Her head swirled. Sherry didn't even have the grace to blush, but Jane did, horribly aware of how they must have looked, their heads close together like conspirators.

'Why, Mr Salgado-Lézille—why don't you join us?'

'Please, Mr Salgado will do. The full name is such a… *mouthful*…if that's the right term.'

Jane cringed, going even pinker with embarrassment, and she marvelled at Sherry's hide, which was as thick as a rhinoceros. He flicked Sherry a dismissive glance and turned his attention to Jane, holding out a hand in a clear invitation to dance. She couldn't refuse. Especially after what had just happened. Wordlessly she put her hand in his much larger one and felt a tingle go up her arm as he lightly guided her onto the dance floor.

Drawing into his arms, Jane fought for composure. The difference between this man and Pete from only a few moments ago was laughable. This was what she had been afraid of—this melting feeling, a hyper-awareness of every part of her skin, an acute consciousness of the way her body seemed to want to fuse with his. His scent was clean and crisp, with a hint of some indefinably erotic element. The man himself, she guessed.

One arm held her securely, high across her back, his hand curving around to just beside her breast. His other hand held hers lightly against his chest. They said nothing, swaying together in perfect unison. When the song ended he held her fast when she would have pulled away until another number started up.

'Don't you think you owe me at least one more dance?'

Jane lifted her head and looked up into his eyes. 'Of…of course.'

His eyes glinted in the flickering light of the candles all around them, a small hard smile playing around his mouth.

As they started to move again she felt she had to say something, blurting out, 'I'm sorry about Sherry... That is, I don't even really know her. I'd hate for you to think that you were the subject of our...' She trailed off, reminding herself that she *had* been listening to Sherry with bated breath. 'I thought you were just one of the pilots...'

Even as the words came out she wanted to grab them back. But it was too late. She couldn't mistake the cynical edge to his voice,

'Ah...I should have known. It is much easier to accept a dance, or dinner for that matter, from the owner of a hotel rather than just a pilot.'

She pulled back as far as he would allow, every line in her body indignant. 'I didn't mean it like that...that had nothing to do with anything, Mr Salgado. The reason I declined your invitation earlier was because—' She broke off. As if she could tell him that the reason she'd turned him down was because her reaction to him had scared the life out of her.

'Well?' he prompted softly, one dark brow lifted.

'I...I, well, as you can see I had made arrangements with Sherry and Brad.' She crossed her fingers, hating the lie, but self-preservation was more important. 'I'm not actually staying here...I'm alone, staying at a friend's villa on the hill. I ended up on the day trip by mistake earlier, and they invited me for dinner.'

It wasn't a complete lie, she reassured herself. Their invitation had just come after his.

He frowned slightly. 'The tour manager told me about someone who had inadvertently ended up on a trip coming in afterwards to pay...was that you?'

'I guess so...unless there was someone else.'

'Quite an enigma, aren't you? Miss...?'

'Vaughan. Jane Vaughan.'

He stepped back for a moment and made a courteous bow, taking her hand. 'Pleased to meet you, Miss Vaughan.'

And then he kissed her hand. She could feel his lips firm and yet soft against her skin, and the fluttering excitement grew stronger in her belly.

'Let's start again,' he said, in a low seductive voice, tucking her into him even closer than before.

Jane fought an internal battle for a few seconds and then gave in. It was too strong…this…whatever it was that she was feeling. She allowed her head to fall into the crook of his neck and shoulder, closing her eyes. A perfect fit.

His hand on her back was moving in slow sensuous circles, grazing her bare skin. She could feel her breasts grow heavier, sensitive against the material of her dress. When he shifted subtly she could feel the thrust of his arousal low against her belly. She pulled back for a second, but Xavier felt it and caught her even closer, growling into her ear, 'You can't move now. Everyone will see what you're doing to me.'

Jane blushed scarlet to the roots of her hair. The next few minutes were an exercise in erotic torture. She had never felt anything like this in her life. Completely unaware of everyone around them. Burning up.

Finally, when she feared her very legs weren't capable of holding her up any more, he pulled back, but held onto her hand. Dark green eyes glittered into blue ones.

'Let's get out of here.'

She nodded mutely. She was being swept away on a tidal wave of feelings and sensations. Sanity tried to break through her consciousness but she pushed it aside. She couldn't let this second chance slip away.

They were in the alcove that led outside to the front of the building and the gardens. Muslin drapes fluttered around them, acting as a shield between the lobby and the main entrance. Jane stopped suddenly. 'Wait!' She turned horrified eyes to his. 'I can't just leave…I'm with people…Pete.'

How could she have forgotten and be so unquestionably rude? No matter what wild spirit seemed to have taken her over, there was no excuse for leaving so abruptly. And, more to the point, the fact that this man had made her take leave of her senses so easily caused a panicky sensation in her belly.

Xavier's eyes narrowed as he looked down at her and took in her expressive face. He had forgotten about her companions too…all he had been aware of was getting her out of there to some private place where he could explore that lush mouth and—

'I'm sorry, Mr Salgado—'

'Xavier, please…'

She couldn't bring herself to say his name. 'I'll have to go back to the others. I really can't just run out on them like this.'

She hoped that the regret in her voice didn't sound too obvious. But the heavy disappointment in her chest dispelled any panic. He'd wouldn't indulge her again. No doubt he thought she must be playing some game with him. She watched with dismay as he seemed to concur.

'You are right. It would be remiss of me to take you away. But be under no illusion that if you weren't obliged to return then right now I would be doing this…'

Before she knew what was happening he had pulled her close, one arm around her back, the other cradling her head, covering her mouth with his. Taking advantage of her startled sigh, he expertly plundered the moist interior, exploring, tracing her lips. When his tongue sought and found hers, stroking with sure mastery, a white-hot flame of desire raced through her body. Her hands clenched on his shoulders in reaction. She was lost in the moment…and in him.

Reluctantly Xavier lifted his head to look down. She took a second to open glazed eyes, lashes long against her cheeks, her lips swollen and parted slightly. He felt the tremor in the body held tightly against his. She would be his, of that he had no doubt. He had branded her.

Jane stepped back and tried to control her breathing, just

managing to stop herself from bringing a hand up to feel her lips. Crazily, she felt as if he had just marked her in some way. She had heard about kisses like that, and thought it was some pathetic fantasy, or Lisa waxing lyrical about her latest obsession…but it wasn't. If he hadn't stopped when he had…

She had been reduced to mush by little more than a kiss.

'Yes…well…I…have to…'

'Have lunch with me tomorrow.'

He still wanted to see her?

She looked at him helplessly. She felt like a moth that was being attracted to a flame with danger written all over it, but the pull was so inexorable that she couldn't help herself. She took a deep breath. The new Jane. Quash the panic. She felt shaky.

'I'd like that.'

'Which villa are you staying at?'

She told him the address.

'*Bien.* I will pick you up at midday…till then.'

He strode back into the lobby and got into the lift without a backward glance.

Jane wandered back out to the poolside table in a daze. Sherry squealed when she saw her arrive. Remarkably, the men still hadn't returned from the bar. Jane felt as though whole lifetimes had passed since Xavier had asked her to dance.

She fielded Sherry's questions, being as vague as possible. When the men arrived back poor Pete didn't stand a chance. He tried to press a kiss to her lips before she left at the end of the evening, but she gave him her cheek. Somehow the thought of anyone else kissing her where Xavier had was anathema.

She didn't see the look of triumph on the face of the man watching from his penthouse suite overlooking the pool.

Back in the villa, Jane couldn't settle and went up to the terrace which overlooked the twinkling lights of the town below, still feeling slightly dazed. Her thoughts drifted to her mother, who she hoped was enjoying much the same view. She was on her honeymoon in Cyprus, with Arthur, the man she'd met a year previously. Jane thought of the recent wedding day with a smile. How proud she had been to give her mother away to such a kind, gentle man. If anyone deserved another stab at happiness it was she.

Since her father had died at just thirty, leaving her mother penniless, with Jane still a baby, it had been a monumental struggle. Her mother had changed overnight from a relatively carefree newlywed to a woman who had had to seek work to make ends meet. Sometimes she worked three jobs at once, just to put food on the table and get Jane through school and then college, despite Jane working too to help out.

Even when Jane had finished her degree and had begun working as a teacher her mother had refused money, insisting that she build up a nest egg for herself.

Years of worry and work had sapped her mother's joy and increased Jane's concern. But now…now she was allowing herself to feel love and happiness again, and if she could embrace a new lease on life then so could Jane.

Starting tomorrow.

With a shiver of anticipation snaking down her spine she finally left the view.

CHAPTER THREE

WHEN she woke the next morning Jane couldn't believe she had slept at all—much less for… She consulted her watch in disbelief—ten hours straight. Which meant, she realised with a lurch of panic, that she had exactly one hour before Xavier was due to pick her up for lunch.

She sprang out of bed and after a quick shower regarded her wardrobe, plucking a pair of white culottes from the messy pile, and a striped white and black halterneck top. She smoothed her hair behind her ears, and with espadrilles and a pair of hoop earrings was just about ready to go downstairs when the doorbell rang.

Already!

She took a few deep breaths and walked to the front door, trying to calm the butterflies in her belly.

Be cool, be calm, be sophisticated.

She opened the door, the smile on her face fading and her mouth going dry when she took in the man in front of her. Pure devastation. He was leaning against the doorframe, arms folded across his broad chest, showing his muscles off to perfection. He wore a casually faded black T-shirt and jeans, scuffed deck shoes on his bare feet. She could feel her face colour as she brought her eyes back up. She had just examined him…and blatantly!

She couldn't see his eyes, as they were hidden behind

dark shades, but she saw all too well the way his mouth quirked.

'I hope I pass inspection?'

What could she do? She had been caught out beautifully. She had to smile, revealing small, even white teeth and a dimple in her cheek.

'You'll do.'

She bent down to pick up her bag, where she'd stuffed her bikini and a sarong among other bits and pieces, not sure what he had planned, and pulled the door behind her, careful to lock it securely. He took the bag from her and led the way to his car. She was glad to see that although it was a convertible it wasn't one of those tiny low-slung things that she privately thought looked ridiculous.

As he negotiated his way down the small winding streets with casual expertise she started to relax and look around. She was very aware of his tanned hands on the wheel, moving to the gear-stick near her leg, and of the long fingers with short square nails. She swallowed and quickly put on the shades that had been resting on her head in case he caught her staring again.

'How long are you here for?' he asked idly.

'Just another week; I've already been here for one. This is such a treat.'

'What is?'

Nerves made her babble. 'To be taken out…driven around. I have a hire car, but this place is like a labyrinth… The first day it took me an hour to find my way back up the hill from the town.'

'I know…it is getting crazier, with more and more tourists… We're hoping that they'll make the centre of the town entirely for pedestrians only; it's small enough, so it could work.'

His comment reminded her who she was dealing with. He wasn't just a local, he was *the* local. She felt intimidated all of a sudden.

He cast a curious glance her way. 'Cat got your tongue?'

She shrugged lightly, honesty prevailing. 'I know this might sound silly, but I keep forgetting that you are…who you are. You own that entire island…that hotel chain. I guess it's just a little overwhelming. I bump into you in the street two days ago and now here I am in your car.' She gave a nervous laugh.

Xavier looked over at her sharply, but she had her face averted. Well, this was a new approach—and one that he hadn't encountered before. Was she for real? More or less hinting that she'd be more comfortable with him if he were just a pilot? He'd never had to reassure a woman before by playing his status down…normally they wanted him to play it up! Well, if this was a game that she was playing then he would play along. She was intriguingly different from any other woman he'd ever known. Whether it was artifice or not he didn't much care. He wasn't planning on getting to know her too well…just well enough.

His glance took in the long shapely legs beside him. He could imagine how they might feel wrapped around his naked back. He grew hard there and then, much to his chagrin. He wasn't used to being at the mercy of hormones he had long ago learnt to control. A woman hadn't had the power to ignite his desire so forcibly since…*ever*, he realised. He focused on the road, hands gripping the wheel. Only one way to exorcise this hunger raging in his blood.

He forced himself to say lightly, 'Ah, so you admit now that you were the one who bumped into me?'

Jane cast him a quick glance, relieved to see him flash her a teasing smile.

Lord, but he was gorgeous. She couldn't answer, nervously touching her tongue to dry lips.

'I thought we'd take a little trip on my boat. I know a cove near here that's usually deserted. We can swim and have a picnic.'

She was going to forget everything and enjoy this moment

for what it was. She was being given a second chance…her fantasy was coming true…and she was smart enough not to sabotage it again. She hoped.

'That sounds lovely.'

After he had parked the car and lifted out a hamper, he led her into a private marina, where yacht after yacht was lined up, bobbing on the water. His was a small sleek speed boat, with a tiny cabin down below.

'This is how you get to and from the island?'

'Yes…or I use the helicopter. This takes fifteen minutes.'

Of course…the helicopter!

It was hard to keep her intimidation at bay when he threw out such admissions of extreme wealth. She forgot everything, though, as he helped her into the boat, big hands curling around her waist to steady her, just under her breasts. Suddenly breathless, she moved away quickly to the other end and looked anywhere but at him. She could see the tourists in the distance, lining up for their day trips. That had been her yesterday, and if she hadn't tagged onto that particular queue…

He showed her where to sit back and relax as he started up the engine and they pulled out into the open water. The breeze felt wonderfully cool on Jane's skin, and she closed her eyes, lifting her face to the sun.

When she opened them again she found Xavier staring at her from behind the wheel, shades on his head. He didn't look away. The gleam in his eyes was explicit, and Jane's pulse started to speed up and throb through her veins. That kiss last night came back in vivid Technicolor, the feel of his chest against hers… She was the one to break contact first, putting on her sunglasses again. His mouth quirked in a mocking smile, the same one he had smiled in the street, aware of his effect. She tried not to let it unsettle her.

Leaving the harbour and marina behind, Xavier hugged the coast for a while. Jane was enthralled by the view of all the huge estates visible from their vantage point. They couldn't really talk over the sound of the engine, but she was happy to drink in the sight of him when she was sure she couldn't be caught. She'd never been reduced to this level of carnal feeling before. Didn't know how to handle it.

She could see a small cove come into view, and Xavier negotiated the boat towards it. It looked empty. She was bizarrely both disappointed and excited not to have company, but if she was honest with herself she knew which feeling won out.

When he had anchored a short way from the shore he indicated the cabin below. 'Why don't you change into your swimsuit here? That way you can leave your things on board.'

'Sure.' Jane feigned a nonchalance that she was far from feeling.

Down below in the small cabin, she changed with awkward haste, half terrified that he'd come down the ladder. Her bikini had felt perfectly adequate up until today, but now she pulled at it ineffectually and tried to stretch it out. Had it shrunk? Somehow it felt as if it had become the skimpiest two-piece on earth since she had last worn it, and she was very conscious of her skin, still pale despite a slight tan. She chastised herself. He was no doubt used to seeing women baring a lot more, especially in this part of the world.

When she emerged from the cabin her skin was still gleaming from an application of suncream. Xavier's breath stopped in his throat as she was revealed bit by bit. Like a lust-controlled youth, he couldn't take his eyes off her chest, full and generous, yet perfectly shaped. She had tied a sarong around hips that flared out gently from a small waist. She looked shy and uncertain, as if she couldn't bring herself to meet his eyes, which were hidden behind his dark lenses. Unbidden, and as swift as his physical response, came a desire to reassure and protect. Alien and unwelcome emotions when it came to him and women. Especially ones he'd known for less than forty-eight hours.

He masked it speaking more brusquely than he'd intended. 'The water should only be waist-deep here, so you can wade ashore.'

He had to stop himself staring when she took off her sarong to reveal a curvy bottom and those never-ending legs... Her self-consciousness was at odds with her body. A body made for pleasure. *His* pleasure.

When Jane hit the water she welcomed the distraction from the fever racing in her blood. Tried to block out the potent image of the man leaning over the edge.

'OK?'

'Yes...fine.'

She half-swam, half-waded to the shore, grateful for the moment to herself. However impressive she had thought his physique while under clothes, it hadn't prepared her for seeing him half naked. He should come with a health warning. He was the most perfect man she had ever seen. She'd tried to avoid looking, but it was impossible not to take in that expanse of bare, toned, exquisitely muscled chest. A light smattering of dark hair led down in a silky line to where his shorts... She gulped as she rested on the sand.

He was wading towards her, with the hamper held aloft in his arms, dark hair gleaming wetly against his head. Strong-muscled legs strode out of the water towards her. She had spread her sarong out on the sand, and was glad of the need for sunglasses and the protection, however slight, they afforded her. She brought her knees up to her chest, wrapping her arms around them in another unconscious gesture of protection.

To her relief, he was businesslike. Coming to rest beside her on the sand, he opened up the basket, taking out a light blanket. He spread it out and started to take out a mouthwatering array of food. Olives, bread, cheese, houmous...sliced ham, chicken wings, pâté.

'There's enough food here to feed an army.'

'Well, I don't know about you, but I'm starving.'

'I wouldn't know where to start.'

'Why don't we start here?' he said, uncorking a bottle of champagne that came in its own encasing to ensure it stayed chilled. He filled two glasses and handed one to her.

'To…meeting you.'

'To meeting you.' She echoed his words, not sure what to say.

A funny feeling lodged in her chest as she took a sip, the bubbles tickling her nostrils. As he busied himself preparing her a selection of food to pick from on a plate, she couldn't help but shake the feeling that this was all a little too smooth…practiced, even—as if he had done it a thousand times before.

'Do you come here often?' she asked lightly, trying to make it sound like a joke.

He stopped what he was doing and looked at her sharply. 'Do you mean have I brought women here before? Then the answer is yes.'

She was taken aback by his honesty. He hadn't tried to temper his words, or make her feel better. Somehow it comforted her. Although the thought of being the latest in a long line of undoubtedly more beautiful women caused some dark emotion to threaten her equilibrium, which she was barely clinging on to as it was.

'I can tell you, though, that it hasn't been for some time. And there probably haven't been half as many as you seem to be imagining. I've come here since my teens, and it's a favourite hang-out for friends of both sexes…not some place purely to seduce women.'

'Oh…well, of course. I never thought for a second—'

'Yes, you did—but I suppose I can't blame you.'

A blush crept up over her face and she turned her attention to the food, hoping to distract him and get off the subject. She could envisage a neon sign above her head with an arrow pointing downwards saying—*Gauche!*

She crossed her legs and helped him to put out the food.

If anything had ever helped her to take her mind off things then it was food. She tucked in healthily. After the first few mouthfuls she looked up to find him staring.

'What?' She wiped her mouth with a napkin. 'Have I got some food somewhere?'

He shook his head, taking his glasses off. 'I don't think I've ever seen a woman eat the way you do. You look like you could keep going until everything is gone.'

She smiled wryly. 'My appetite is legendary, I'm afraid. You've probably met your match. I've never been a delicate eater…'

He nodded towards her. 'Keep going, please—I'm enjoying the novelty of watching a woman relish her food.'

Suddenly self-conscious, she took a sip of champagne to wet her throat and forced herself to keep eating as nonchalantly as possible. But now his attention was focused on her it was impossible. He seemed to be fixated by her mouth. She swallowed a piece of cheese with difficulty.

'The history of your island seems fascinating…what I read of it in the exhibit space. Has your family really been there for centuries?'

Thankfully he finally took his gaze away. 'Yes. They were given the island as a gift by the French royal family in the twelfth century. We originally came from Aragon, in Spain. The royals in the north wanted to establish allies in the south. We took the name of the island and added it to Salgado… hence my name today.'

'And are there many in your family now?'

His voice was curiously unemotional. 'No, just me left… Hard to believe that the line could very well die out with me. I was the first born, and my mother passed away when I was five…my father never married again, and he died when I was in my early twenties.'

Jane pushed her glasses up onto her head, her eyes wide and sympathetic. 'I'm sorry…he must have loved her a great deal…and to lose both parents so young… My father died when I was small too—a baby. But at least I still have my mother.'

Xavier looked into her eyes and felt an unfamiliar sensation, almost like losing his footing. How had they got onto this subject?

She gazed out to the sea and shook her head.

'I just remembered what I read about the earthquake…it must have affected your family?'

He followed her look. 'Yes, it did…all of them perished apart from my great-grandparents…not to mention many of the islanders. Whole families were wiped out.'

'That's awful. It must have taken generations to begin to forget, rebuild lives…'

He nodded. 'We built a commemorative grotto to their memory on the island some years ago. There are hundreds of names inscribed.'

She turned shining eyes on him, stunning him again momentarily. 'That sounds like a lovely thing to do. I wish I'd seen it…how come the tour didn't go there?'

He shrugged. 'It's small, and wouldn't mean much to anyone else. It's a very personal space for the islanders.'

He regarded her profile. 'If you want you could come back there with me tomorrow and I'll show it to you.'

'Would you really?'

She couldn't control the surge of excitement that took hold at the thought of seeing him again the next day.

He nodded. They didn't speak for a few moments, and then he started to pack away some food but refilled her glass. He avoided her eye.

'I'm going for a quick swim, but you should let your food settle for a while.'

She had to smile inwardly at his arrogant assumption that he was somehow immune to cramp after eating. Which, she had to admit as she watched his powerful back and legs walk away from her, he probably was. Immune to banal mortal complaints.

She lay back on her sarong, feeling deliciously relaxed and replete. The sky was hazy, the sun blissfully not beating down with full force. The lapping of the waves lulled her into a light sleep.

A while later she woke with a start… She looked to her side, to see Xavier stretched out beside her. The basket was gone and there was nothing between them. His eyes were closed, lashes long and dark against high cheekbones. He really was beautiful.

'Do I pass inspection again?' he asked, opening one eye, fixing her.

She sat up quickly to hide her mortification. 'I think I'll go for a swim now…'

'I'll join you.' And with lithe grace he stood up beside her and held out a hand. She looked at it warily for a moment before taking it.

The initial cool of the waves lapping against her feet woke her up better than a pail of water over her head.

She extricated her hand from his, and once in far enough dived headlong into the first big wave, swimming underwater for as long as her breath held out.

She popped up to the surface some way off and shook her head. The sun glinting off the water was dazzling. She looked around and could see Xavier's sleek head, arms gracefully scissoring through the water as he swam powerfully towards her. She trod water, breathing far more heavily than was normal after what she had just done.

He came within a couple of feet of her. They just looked at each other. Simultaneously his arms reached for her, and she felt herself gravitate towards him as if being pulled by a magnetic force until she was in his arms. It felt completely right…inevitable.

He brought her arms around his neck and instinctively she wrapped her legs around his waist to steady herself. She was out of her depth…in more ways than one.

Seduced by the place, by him, and her resolve to embrace the moment, she gave in to a powerful desire. Slowly she dipped her head towards his, eyes closing as she felt the hard, sensual contours of his lips. His arms were like a steel band around her waist.

With naive boldness she explored his lips, feeling their shape and texture. One of his hands moved up to the back of her head and he angled it, his tongue sliding between her lips to taste and explore. Hesitantly she allowed him access.

A molten urgent feeling was building between her legs, the centre of her desire. She could feel the friction against his chest, and just below her bottom she could feel a hard ridge. Realizing what it was made her gasp.

He tore his lips from hers and looked down. Her nipples were two hard points thrusting against the wet material of her bikini.

He brought smoky green eyes up to hers and shifted her subtly, so that now he carried her in his arms and out of the water.

Jane knew that if he had put her down her legs would have given way, and was thankful he didn't as he walked up the beach and laid her down on the sarong, stretching out his long length beside her. He looked down her body, a hand resting possessively on her stomach, its gentle feminine swell.

'So beautiful...'

'So are you,' she said shyly.

The sun was blocked as his head dipped again to take her mouth, slowly, languorously. As if they had all the time in the world to touch, explore. She arched herself towards him slightly, a hand reaching out blindly to rest against his chest, revelling in the feel of the surprisingly silky hair, finding a hard nipple, circling it experimentally before flicking it accidentally with a nail.

He tore his mouth away with a moan. 'Let's see how *you* like that.'

Before she could question what he was doing, he had lowered his mouth to one jutting peak, sucking through the wet material of her top. An exquisite burst of pleasure made her cry out. He was relentless, and she gasped when he finally pulled the material aside to reveal the dark peak, raw and aroused. The feel of his tongue on her bare skin made her almost pass out with pleasure, and then he moved to the other side.

Jane barely recognised this wanton version of herself. Her hands tangled in his hair, holding his head in case he might pull away. She was caught up…caught up in uncharted territory…powerless to do anything but feel…respond.

She could feel him drifting a hand down over her belly, to rest near the top of her briefs. Toying with her, moving in slow sensuous circles, before his fingers moved down…under the elastic, over the mound of soft hair…down further, until…

She held her breath, her body tensing as his fingers dipped into her most secret place, exploring, rubbing back and forth over the most sensitive part, which she could feel getting slicker, harder. It was too much. No one had ever touched her there.

Her legs came together, trapping his hand, but he gently manoeuvred them apart again.

A very strident child-like squeal made them both tense.

In a haze of pleasure that was fast receding Jane became aware of Xavier reacting quicker than her, adjusting her bikini back over her body, which felt acutely sensitised.

'We have company…pity,' he drawled, making sure she was decent again, and then he looked down into her shocked eyes.

Sure enough another boat was pulling into the small cove, and a gang of children were starting to jump down from a yacht into the water, splashing and swimming towards the beach. Thankfully they were far enough out not to have seen anything…she hoped.

She wanted the sand to rise up around her and suck her

down. A mortified flush burned her skin as she thought of what would have happened if they hadn't arrived. He must think her so...easy. Bring her to a deserted stretch of beach, ply her with a little champagne and food, and she was a possessed woman in his arms, with little or no encouragement. The worst cliché of a tourist looking for a quick holiday fling.

She thrust herself away from him and sat up, gathering her sarong around her waist and tying it in a knot.

'This has been...lovely...but we probably should be getting back. I'm sure you have lots of important things to be doing.'

She couldn't even look at him. She stood up awkwardly and a soft gasp escaped her lips as she felt him whirl her around to face him. She couldn't escape his eyes, which probed far deeper than the surface. They were oblivious to the people arriving onto the beach only feet away from them.

'Lovely...?' He shook his head incredulously. 'Correct me if I'm wrong, but if we hadn't been interrupted, right about now I think you would be fast approaching a climax.'

She blanched at the starkness of his words.

'*Lovely* is a little bit of an understatement, don't you think, for what two people seem to be able to ignite in each other within seconds or with just a look?'

'I...I...well, maybe...'

His eyes were hypnotic. 'The most important thing on my mind at the moment is exploring this attraction between us.'

'It is?'

'Yes.'

'Look...Xavier...we hardly know each other, and I'm not normally—'

'So responsive? Well, neither am I.' His voice sounded harsh.

She had been about to say *easy*, and amended her words. 'That is...I mean...I want you to know that it wasn't my intention to come here just for some kind of holiday...thing.'

He moved her closer to him, looping deceptively loose

arms around her waist, ignoring the chatter around them. She came in contact with the still semi-hard evidence of his arousal. Immediately an answering liquid heat pooled in her groin.

'And, contrary to what you may think, I'm not in the habit of pursuing random tourists…I'm not sure what this is either, but don't you think it might be fun to explore?'

Fun. Explore. The words resounded in her head.

He stepped back, putting her away from him gently. 'I'll take you back now, but I have a proposition…' He trailed a long finger down one cheek. 'I promised to bring you to the island tomorrow to show you the memorial.'

He lifted a brow as if to ask if she still wanted to do that.

She felt herself nodding slowly, trying to focus just on his words, not on the finger caressing her heated skin.

'I'd like you to come and stay there as my guest for the rest of the week… We could get to know one another… explore this…attraction.' His finger left her cheek. 'It's up to you.'

He looked at her for a long moment, before shading his eyes again with the dark glasses and starting back towards the boat. He hadn't meant to ask her to stay, the words had surprised him, but now, having asked, it felt right. One thing was for sure. An afternoon picnic wasn't enough.

A few seconds later Jane followed blindly, her mind churning furiously. She would never see him again after this week. She would have it to hug to herself for ever. What did she have to lose? Could she really be contemplating this? Could she indulge the fantasy?

They were silent on the boat back, and during the car journey up to the villa. He was detached and polite. At her front door they looked at one another for the first time since they had left the beach. He tipped up her face with a finger under her chin.

'So, Jane Vaughan…I'll be here to pick you up at ten a.m. It can be a simple day trip to see the grotto, or you can come and stay for the next few days… Like I said, the choice is yours.'

And then he was in his car, the purring sound of the engine growing fainter before she drew in another breath, still looking at the spot where he had stood. She knew without a doubt that he would let her go at the end of the next day if she so desired. He was far too proud to push her. It was, as he'd said, up to her.

She mechanically went into the house, and before she knew what she was doing she realised that she was packing her things, tidying up in readiness to leave for a few days. Her body was ahead of her brain. She sat on the couch in the living room, an excited, nervous, shivery feeling in her belly.

Be careful what you wish for because you just might get it. The words popped into her head. Well, this was what she had wished for, wasn't it? The start of something new. Letting go of the old reliable, sensible, mature Jane. It was time for her to have some fun for a change. And when someone like Xavier Salgado-Lézille wanted you…then surely it went against the flow of the universe to say no? She was being offered a taste of something that she knew many women would not hesitate for a second to experience.

The only thing was…she had a sneaking suspicion that more than her body was in danger of falling under his spell. Was it a risk she was prepared to take? A resounding voice in her head said *yes*. Throw caution to the wind. She caught sight of her reflection in a mirror. I mean really, she asked herself, how involved could she get in one week? She turned away before she could see the mocking glint in her eye.

CHAPTER FOUR

By NINE forty-five the next morning Jane was having second, third and fourth thoughts. In the cold light of day things were more stark. She would get burned. And not from the sun. She knew it. She heard an engine outside. He was early. As if he could hear the doubts that were in her private thoughts. Which was ridiculous.

She took a deep breath and waited for the doorbell to sound. She was wearing simple shorts, flip-flops and a plain T-shirt. If he wanted her then he could have her as she was, unadorned.

She lifted the small weekend bag that she had brought to carry home gifts, and suddenly it felt as if it held rocks instead of clothes and toiletries for the next few days.

The doorbell rang. Her heart stopped. She could see his tall dark shape against the glass. The Prince of Darkness. The name made her shiver.

When she opened the door his sharp eyes took in her slender figure in the plain clothes, and the bag clutched in one hand with her knuckles showing white. Instinctively he schooled his features, not allowing the surge of triumph he felt to show on his face. For once in his life he actually hadn't been sure which way a woman was going to react, and had been prepared for her to reject his offer. But the bag told him that she was saying yes. He needed to tread carefully. She was as skittish as a colt. He bent to take the bag from her grip, and left her to lock up.

Jane had sent a text to Lisa that morning, wishing her all the best for her dad's operation and saying she was taking a small trip. Just in case Lisa rang and got no answer from the house. She wasn't going to go into any details about Xavier yet. If her friend thought for a second there was a man in the picture she'd be like a dog with a bone.

And, as Jane could barely quantify to herself what was happening, she could hardly begin to explain herself to someone else.

By the time they reached the island, and Xavier had guided her to a waiting Jeep, she had pushed any last dissenting voices out of her head. He was being a complete gentleman. Charming, funny, insightful. She hadn't felt this kind of connection with anyone before—almost as though they'd known each other for years.

A couple of times when they'd locked eyes the heat had flared, swift and intense, reminding her of what was not so far from the surface.

He paused in the Jeep, turning towards her in his seat. 'We'll have to go to my home first…an unavoidable conference call I need to take. My penance for taking some time off…I'm sorry.'

'That's OK…I don't mind.'

'So, what I was going to suggest was this…as it's nearly lunch, why don't we eat, you can get settled, and we see the memorial tomorrow?'

This was it. Even though he was assuming that she wanted to stay, he was giving her the opportunity to back out now. But she didn't want to. She had to take the chance, knowing that in her acceptance, should she choose it, he would read her total acquiescence. She took a deep breath, feeling as though she were stepping over an invisible line drawn in the sand.

'All right. That sounds good.'

He looked at her for a long moment before leaning over and placing a feather-light kiss on her lips. 'It will be, Jane…are you sure?'

She looked at him steadily. 'Yes, I'm sure.'

With a spurt of dry earth, he turned the Jeep towards the castle in the distance. After they came to a stop in the courtyard outside, Jane couldn't hide her reaction. It didn't look like a castle, in the sense of turrets and moats. It had two higher wings on either side, huge, imposing archways, and intricate carvings on every stone. She had never seen anything like it before.

'It's amazing… Sorry—I'm sure you get that all the time. But really it is beautiful.'

Xavier had stepped out of the Jeep and looked up, hands on hips. 'Yes, I guess it is…the Moorish influence probably makes it a little less austere.'

'I thought that was what it was, when I saw it from the distance the other day, but I wasn't sure.'

He lifted out her bag and took her hand, leading her into a huge open-plan flagstoned hall covered in complicated mosaics. Numerous green plants stood against the walls, and the open spaces were light-filled and indescribably foreign and exotic. Tall pillars led to an inner roofless courtyard.

Jane looked around in awe, taking it all in. She could almost imagine an ancestor of Xavier's reclining darkly on a divan, voluminous folds of silk covering his body, being attended to by lustrous haired beauties. She blushed at her imagination. Xavier reached out a finger and trailed it down her cheek, leaving a line of fire in its wake.

'You blush so easily…a rare phenomenon these days.'

'An embarrassing one, you mean…it tends to come at the most awkward moments, when the last thing I want is for someone to guess I might be unnerved.'

'And are you…unnerved…here, now, with me?'

'Well…a little.'

'Your honesty is refreshing. How have you managed not to lose it yet?'

'That's a very cynical thing to say.'

'I've come to learn it's a very cynical world we live in...but you might prove me wrong.'

Her eyes widened, a vulnerable light in their depths. That and any other thought flew from her mind as his large body closed the distance between them and he claimed her mouth with a kiss full of pent-up passion, his hands moving over her back. She found herself responding, instinctively matching his passion with her own.

Before she knew what was what, she felt herself being lifted into strong arms, and hers automatically went around his neck as he walked back into the hall and up some stairs which were obscured behind material moving gently in the breeze.

She took in an upper level, corridors, more open spaces, before Xavier shouldered his way through an imposing oak door and into a vast room, with a huge king-size bed in the centre. She barely had time to take in the rest of the room before he put her on her feet. Sudden panic gripped her. This was happening too quickly. She backed away, breath coming hard and fast.

'Wait...do you think we could just...take things slowly for now?'

He stood back from her and ran a hand through his hair. When he saw the look on her face he said quickly, 'I never planned on dragging you up here like some teenager...I just lost control...which seems to happen more and more frequently since I saw you.'

He gave her a rueful smile. He held out a hand and she took it.

'Come on. Let's have some lunch, and I promise not to manhandle you again.'

'That's OK. It's not that I don't *want* to be manhandled by you. I'm sure that'd be perfectly nice—'

'Jane.'

'Yes?'

'Stop talking. It's fine, you don't have to say anything.'

'OK.'

He paused at a door almost opposite his bedroom, opening it to reveal another equally stunning room.

'This is your room. I'll bring your bag up after we've eaten and you can get settled.' He turned towards her. 'I'm sorry again, Jane. Believe me, I didn't just assume that because you're staying falling into my bed is a foregone conclusion, but I won't lie to you…I want you. I'm perfectly happy for us to take it slowly, get to know each other…I'll wait until you're ready'

Her heart flipped over. Danger. She looked up into his eyes, feeling a drowning sensation, 'Thank you…'

He needed the space as much as she did. The truth was that he had never before felt such an overwhelming urge to take a woman to his bed… His plan, as he had told her, had been that they would have lunch, get to know one another a little better, have dinner in the evening and then…who knew? But within mere minutes of coming in the front door he had been overtaken by his hormones.

People called him the Prince of Darkness. Because in business he was ruthless and brilliant—even cold, some would say, but always fair. He had that necessary detachment. It was the same with women. He was the one in control. Always. Without exception. Until now.

Jane sat back a while later, in her chair at the lunch table Xavier had set up in the inner courtyard. He had made a light meal of gazpacho soup with a summer salad and crusty bread, all washed down with a crisp white wine.

'That was delicious…I don't think I've eaten as well in months.'

'Like I said yesterday, it's a pleasure to see a woman enjoy her food, and I like cooking.'

'You'd better be careful or you might be rolling me out of here in a few days.'

She smiled easily, but the words reminded her that this *was* only for a few days. A mere interlude. Xavier would never remember someone like her when this was over. He would be moving on to the next exquisite beauty. Someone much more his equal, in every way.

'You have such an expressive face…'

She groaned with a lightness she suddenly didn't feel. 'That along with the blushing…it must be an intoxicating mix for someone used to a more sophist—'

He shook his head, cutting her off. 'Don't even say it…you have more innate grace in you than half the people I deal with every day.'

'Th…thank you.' Her tongue felt heavy in her mouth. She wasn't used to compliments. Wanting to change to subject, she asked, 'Do you have any staff? Surely you can't look after this place by yourself.'

'Yes, I do but they're on a few days' break.'

She couldn't help a silly flutter of fear.

Xavier read the look on her face effortlessly. 'They go on holiday this time every year. It's pure coincidence that it happens to be this week.'

'Oh…of course.'

The fact that he seemed to be able to read her better than anyone she knew made the flutter come back. That was nearly more disturbing than the thought of being alone with him in this huge castle.

'Come on, I'll show you around.'

He stood and held out a hand again, and she found herself taking it without thinking.

Every corner they turned made her exclaim anew. It was full of nooks and crannies, and secret courtyards overflowing with plants and eclectic furniture. She could imagine it being a children's paradise…and immediately stopped her wayward mind. What on earth had made her think of that?

He brought her to a swimming pool at the back. It was surrounded by trees and flowering bushes, in idyllic seclusion from the rest of the house.

'Why don't you go for a swim and relax for a bit? I've got that call to take.'

'OK…why not? If I can ever find my way back here.'

'There are cabins just behind the trees.' He indicated to the other side of the pool. 'Help yourself to a bathing suit and towels; there are robes as well.'

She should have guessed.

She chose a modest one-piece in dark blue, and went back to the pool to choose a lounger. After a quick dip and drying off she succumbed to the peace, which was broken only by the sound of birds and crickets.

A couple of hours later there was still no sign of him, and Jane felt she wanted to wash and get rid of the stickiness of the day. She gathered up her things and tied a robe securely around herself, wandering back through the house until she eventually found the stairs. She whirled around at the sound of a door opening. Xavier stood framed in the doorway. She could see a vast room behind him, with all manner of hi-tech office equipment.

'I'm sorry, but I'm still caught up with this call… Make yourself at home. I shouldn't be much longer.'

'Oh, don't worry about me,' Jane declared airily.

Up in the bedroom, she found her bag and padded barefoot to the *en suite* bathroom. She looked at the huge bath. The bath of her dreams. Filling it almost to the top, and adding copious amounts of the oils and scents that she'd found in a cupboard, she sank blissfully into the bubbles. Along with food, baths were her only other fatal weakness. This one was so huge she could have almost done a length.

But before she could turn into a prune—or, more disturbingly, have Xavier come looking for her—she stepped out. She smoothed on some body lotion and wrapped a towel around herself. Despite it being her own room, she went out cautiously. She couldn't hear any sounds…he must be busy still.

She caught sight of her reflection in a mirror and stopped for a second. She nearly didn't recognise herself. Skin glowing a light golden, her hair drifting around her face in waves, softening the harsh bob it had been when she'd first got it cut. Her eyes shone and sparkled, and her cheeks were flushed rosy from the bath.

In the mirror behind her a figure materialised in the doorway. Her eyes lifted, and she froze and watched as Xavier crossed the room to stand behind her.

Their eyes met in the mirror. There was only the sound of their breathing in the room. His hands were on her shoulders, dark against her skin. She watched, barely able to breathe, as they moved down her arms. She brought her eyes back up to his. Her whole body seemed to be pulsating in time with her heart, goosebumps making her skin prickle in anticipation. Right at that moment she wanted nothing more than for him to read her mind, undo her towel, let it drop to the floor, baring her to his gaze. She wanted him to take her breasts in his dark hands, weigh them, feel their heaviness, she wanted him to take off his clothes so she could lean back against the naked length of him…

But he didn't. His hands came up to her shoulders and rested there heavily.

'I'm sorry it took so long… When you're dressed come back downstairs and I'll cook us some dinner.'

She nodded at his reflection in the mirror, wordlessly watched as he stepped back and away. Thank God he *couldn't* read her mind, she thought shakily as he disappeared. Talk about waking a hitherto dormant sexual desire. Where had those images come from?

She went to close the door and whisked off the towel abruptly, studiously avoiding her own reflection again. In the space of a few hours she had morphed from shrinking virgin to mentally stripping him…but he was taking her at her word, holding back, letting her get comfortable. Well, she'd asked for it. She just hoped that he would take the initiative again, before she had to drum up the courage to let him know that she was ready!

A while later Jane sipped from a glass of deep red wine in the open-plan kitchen as she watched Xavier prepare a simple pasta dish. He was dressed casually, in jeans and a loose shirt, and she was equally casual, in a loose pair of linen trousers and a crossover short-sleeved top. She enjoyed watching him move dexterously around the kitchen.

'Where did you learn to cook?'

He glanced up briefly. 'In my teens I rebelled against the role my father wanted me to take up in the family business—namely the island—and ran away to the flight school on the mainland…I worked as a cook in a restaurant to help pay my way.'

'That's why you took part in the display?'

'Yes…I allow the pilots to do it here every year. Since my father died, we've incorporated it into a summer fête. It's a day out for everyone, and it's good for morale—and it allows me to indulge my love for flying.'

Jane had to suppress a slight shudder when she remembered his death-defying stunts.

'You were better then any of the others…you had some edge that they don't.'

He looked at her, but instead of finding a look of false flattery on her face saw she was busily picking at a salad. She had merely stated a fact.

'Thank you… I do miss it, but it was never going to be my destiny. Once my father died, I had to come back and take over the reins here. It used to be just the vineyard, but I developed abroad into the hotel chain and various other investments…mainly property.'

'Did you see your father before he died?' she asked softly.

'No.' It was curt, and Jane knew she'd hit a nerve. She deflected his attention.

'Well, this all looks more than fabulous—if that's possible. You'll have to let me cook for you, maybe tomorrow…'

He placed a swift kiss on her lips. 'For now, I'm quite happy to cook and enjoy watching you eat.'

For a moment he seemed as shocked as she was at the impulsive kiss that had come so naturally, but he recovered himself quickly.

Jane coloured as he had known she would. How was it that he felt as though he could read her like a book?

They sat out on a veranda at the back of the house. Soft jazz was coming from a speaker that was artfully hidden. Low lights from the house and candles illuminated the scene outside. Steps led down to a beautifully manicured lawn, teeming with exotic flowers. A clear sky glittered with stars and a full moon hung low in the horizon. It was magical.

The conversation flowed as Jane told him about her mother, the marriage, her job…her life. Instead of a glazed look of boredom passing over his face, as she had feared, he seemed genuinely interested.

He cradled his glass of wine. 'It's a strange connection to have…'

When she lifted a quizzical brow he elaborated.

'You growing up without a father, me without a mother.'

Jane nodded and shrugged lightly. 'I know…I wish I'd known him. But you can't really miss what you never had. I think for years Mum immortalised him as the perfect husband, but the truth was that he left us with nothing, and that…that was hard.'

'The truth usually is…'

She was surprised by the bleak look that crossed his face but then it was gone.

He leant forward to top up her glass of wine. 'Enough of this maudlin talk…'

He deftly changed the subject and she found herself forgetting about his enigmatic look as he effortlessly charmed her. After they had exhausted several topics, she couldn't remember when she had enjoyed talking to anyone as much. When she could forget for a moment the intense attraction that was always humming between them…

Later, when he stood and held out a hand to lead her inside, she took it easily. She followed him upstairs to her bedroom door. In the moonlit hallway she could just make out his eyes, feeling them rove over her face. Surely he would…?

She wanted him to take her, mould her to him, kiss her senseless. Her hands itched to pull his head down to hers. But she was too shy to show him. He bent his head and pressed a friendly kiss to her forehead…she felt a crushing disappointment.

'Goodnight, sweet Jane… I'll see you in the morning.' And he firmly turned her towards the bedroom and pushed her gently in.

Hours later Jane lay in sheets that were a tangled mess around her overheated body. Overheated because of all the images that wouldn't abate. Because of the knowledge that that man was mere feet away, probably naked, just lying there… All she had to do was get up, walk over…

She veered between just about getting up and sinking back into the pillows. At one point she cursed him. He probably knew exactly what he was doing, was so tuned in to the female psyche that this was a tried and tested technique… He was probably sleeping like a baby. As the first fingers of dawn crept into the sky she gave up and admitted defeat. She was a coward. Tomorrow, after all, was another day. And it was her own fault. She finally fell into a deep, dreamless sleep of exhaustion.

* * *

Jane woke to a gentle prodding, opening up one eye to see a cleanshaven and impeccable Xavier looking down at her. Both eyes snapped open.

'What time is it?'

'Almost midday…couldn't you sleep last night?'

She eyed him suspiciously from under her lashes, was that a mocking smile? She as good as had *sexual frustration* tattooed on her forehead.

'Fine, thank you, actually…and you?' she asked sweetly, making sure the sheet was pulled all the way up to her neck. Did he *have* to stand so close to the bed?

'Oh…like the proverbial log. I've made a picnic. There's a nice route we can take on the boat to get around to the memorial. We can take a gentle hike up to see it. It's a little more demanding, but ultimately rewarding.'

With a glint in his eye and his lip twitching he took his leave to let her get ready, before she could make a smart comeback to his none too subtle *double entendre*.

Gentle hike…? Some gentle hike, she thought about two hours later, when her legs were aching and sweat was running in rivulets down her brow, between her breasts and down her back. Her shorts and vest clung to her body like an indecent second skin, and all she could do was focus on Xavier's feet ahead of her, making sure to take exactly the same steps as him.

They had come around to the other end of the island, with Xavier pointing out landmarks, interesting birds and fauna along the way. There was so much more than she had seen at first. It was vibrant with the colour of thousands of wild flowers, cared for laboriously by the islanders who grew them to sell on the mainland.

They had docked the boat at a small cove, not dissimilar to the one he had taken her to the other day. He'd pointed up at what looked a perilously long way away to an overhanging rock. She hadn't been able to see the memorial, but he'd assured her that it was up there.

They had left their picnic in the shade on the beach, and now she was following Xavier up the hill, which was fast becoming her personal Everest.

Finally, just when she was about to beg for a break, his feet disappeared. She lifted her head to see his outstretched hand and took it gratefully, allowing him to haul her up the last couple of feet. He didn't let go of her hand, waiting until she had her breath under control, but the view was threatening to take it away again. They had emerged at the highest point of the island, the southernmost tip, and falling away from them and to the north they could see everything…the mainland shimmering faintly in the distance and the castle a small speck up at the other tip.

'This is…words fail me,' she breathed when she had enough to spare.

'I know…it's beautiful, isn't it?'

'Beautiful doesn't do it justice. It's epic…and it's yours.' She shook her head. 'How must it feel to come up here and know that all you survey is yours and yours alone?'

'Not everything…'

She turned her head to see him looking at her. Words crammed her mouth, wanting to come out, but she couldn't say them. She was tongue-tied, wanting to make some flip comment…but it just wasn't her.

He drew her attention to the grotto-like shrine a few feet to their left. It was a simple altar, with some candles, and vases with flowers that looked a few days old. It was sheltered on three sides by walls and a roof, facing out to the sea. She felt immeasurably honoured to be shown this special place. She took the small backpack off her shoulders and reached in, pulling out some flowers she had picked on their way up the hill, placing them in one of the vases. Around at the back, Xavier pointed out where the names were inscribed in clear and simple black paint.

'Thank you for showing me this…it's very special.' Her voice was husky.

'My pleasure.'

He made sure she drank some water, and after a few minutes of companionable silence he took her hand again and started to lead her back down the rocky path.

When they reached the beach Jane saw the water glinting and shimmering, and it was the best thing she'd ever seen. She tore off her shorts and vest, thankful that she had thought to put her bikini on before they left, and ran into the water, relishing the first cool sting and freshness over her sticky body.

Xavier did the same, and she squealed with delight when he emerged from underneath the water only inches away, pulling her down playfully. She silently urged him to kiss her, as he had done that first day, but he was still being the consummate gentleman—much to her growing frustration.

When they were cooled down, he led her back to the beach and spread out a delicious feast. Jane relaxed back and watched him talk…not even hearing his words. She couldn't remember a time when she had felt so full of delighted expectation. She was aware of every part of him—his hands, his mouth, legs…that chest. She was burning up just thinking about touching him, having him touch her. Her skin itched to be next to his. She wanted to reach over, stop his mouth with hers, run her hands over his muscles. But she didn't.

It was as if there was a silent communication going on between them on a subliminal level:

Come on, touch me if you dare…you're the one who wanted to go slowly…

I know! I just don't know what to do…how to make the move.

The atmosphere that surrounded them was thick with it.

That evening her skin felt hot after the sun…or else her imagination was just keeping it overheated. In bare feet and a plain shift dress, she padded down to the kitchen where she could hear Xavier making dinner. She paused at the door, drinking him in as he worked. He wore a white T-shirt and faded jeans, feet bare like hers. His hair was still wet from the shower, like hers, and a crisp fresh scent intoxicated her nostrils as he moved. He looked up then, and caught her staring. She didn't even blush…she was beyond that…just smiled.

His eyes boldly appraised her as she came towards him. She was completely unconscious of the provocatively innocent sway to her hips. He poured her a glass of wine and lifted his to hers. They clinked glasses.

'*À nous.*'

She nodded jerkily in response.

All through dinner they talked, but it had a hushed, frantic quality. A breathless anticipation was building in Jane's belly.

When he stood to take her hand under the stars at the end of the evening she was trembling, unable to speak. They stopped once again outside her door. She turned her face up to his. Wordlessly she tried to communicate with him. Couldn't he tell? Surely he had to know how ready she was? She watched as he brought her hand to his mouth and pressed a kiss to the delicate underside of her wrist. She closed her eyes and felt a weakening in her body, her blood slowing to a deep throbbing pulse.

'Goodnight, Jane. Sleep tight.'

CHAPTER FIVE

GOODNIGHT, Jane…Sleep tight?

Her eyes flew open. *No!* her mind screamed…he had let her hand go. A dark, bottomless pit threatened to suck her down. She had to do something. But even as she thought this, she could feel herself turning away, sudden doubts assailing her. Maybe he didn't find her attractive any more? Maybe he was regretting having asked her to stay? Surely he would have tried to make love to her again?

Then she stopped. She realised that she hadn't heard him move behind her. She turned around slowly and saw his face. It told her everything she needed to know. Raw masculine arousal was stamped into every line. She felt every cell in her body jump in response.

'Xavier—' Her words were stopped as he hauled her into his arms. The relief made her dizzy as she locked her arms around his neck.

'I swear if you had gone into that room I was going to come after you, ready or not…'

'Thank God…because I nearly did…'

'I couldn't have spent another night in that bed, knowing you were only feet away.'

'I nearly went to you last night, but couldn't work up the nerve…'

'What? Do you know how hard it's been for me to keep from touching you all day?'

He groaned and bent his head to hers, finding and taking her lips, tasting them as if they were succulent fruits. His control was fast slipping as his hands smoothed down her back, down to her buttocks, moulding their peachy firmness, cupping them and drawing her up into the cradle of his lap, where he felt her gasp against his mouth when she felt his arousal.

In one graceful move he lifted her against his chest and kicked open his bedroom door, bringing her inside. He brought her over to the mirror, where he stood her in front of him. She looked at him in the reflection, a question on her face.

'This is what I thought of last night, the image that kept me awake.'

She felt his hands at the top of her dress, fingers grazing her skin as he slowly started to pull the zip down. Immediately she knew what he meant, and the thought of him imagining the same scenario made her knees weak.

She felt the slight night breeze on her skin, and shivered in reaction as he gently but firmly pulled the dress from her shoulders and down, past her breasts, past her waist, over the swell of her hips, until it hit the floor with a muted swish. Her bra quickly followed, and she was standing there naked but for a pair of very brief briefs. She brought her hands up to cover her breasts, feeling shy, but he came close behind her and brought them back down.

'Look at how beautiful you are.'

His head lowered and he pressed a hot kiss to where her neck and shoulder met, causing a shudder to run through her body…and then began to shed his own clothes behind her. She could hear the whisper of his T-shirt dropping to the floor, a button being snapped, jeans falling. An unbearable tightness began to build in her abdomen as she continued to watch through their reflection, until he stood behind her completely naked, his dark form a contrast to her much paler one.

Her head felt light. She watched in the mirror as his hands came around her to cup her breasts. They looked full and heavy in his palms. Her eyes widened as she saw her nipples growing harder, puckering, felt the ache that escaped as a guttural moan when his hands closed over them, her nipples caught between his fingers. She could feel his arousal against her bottom and instinctively moved back and leant against him, delighting in his own low moan.

He turned her to face him, bringing her into intimate contact with his whole length, taking her mouth with his. His hands were under her panties, slowly tugging them down until they fell at her feet.

She started to shake uncontrollably with reaction as he lifted her into his arms and walked over to the bed.

He gently laid her down, following her, leaning over her with strong arms. He bent to take her lips, the kiss starting out gentle, rapidly becoming more heated and passionate. Jane's hands stretched out blindly, searching for and finding his chest, his shoulders, smoothing, touching every part she could reach.

He groaned softly as her hands reached lower, coming dangerously close to his rock-hard erection. He couldn't remember ever being so aroused. He shifted to lie down beside her, lifting his head for a moment, watching her reaction as his fingertips closed over one nipple, how her back arched, her eyes closed and her breathing became fractured. Noticing how her skin had flushed to a dull red. He bent and took the jewel-hard peak into this mouth, his own control fast slipping as he suckled and nipped gently, first at one, then the other.

'Xavier… I can't… God!'

Her hands clutched at his shoulders, and her body writhed as he moved a hand down over her belly to feel how ready she was. The wetness he felt at the apex of her thighs almost pushed him over the edge, and he'd hardly touched her! Or she him…

As his hand explored, stroked, Jane felt herself bucking.

She'd had no idea it could be like this. Had had no expectation…certainly hadn't expected this hunger in her blood that was consuming her to the point where she was no longer herself. She had become…someone else? Or perhaps the person she was meant to be… All these incoherent fevered thoughts raced through her head at the same time.

Xavier's fingers were pushing her to a point of no return, his mouth was on hers, then on her breast. It was too much…her whole body stilled for a moment before she felt herself crashing over the edge and tumbling down, her body contracting and pulsating in the aftermath. His hand cupped her mound, waiting until her tremors had stopped. She looked up into his face, her eyes wide with shock… Words trembled on her lips, but then he claimed her mouth once more, with a hot, drugging kiss, and she felt him move over her body. He lifted his head, his eyes glittering in the half-light, pupils dilated with barely contained passion. She sucked in a breath of anticipation as she took in the daunting size of him, moisture beading at the tip.

His voice was hoarse with need and restraint. 'Jane…I can't wait.'

Moving instinctively, she nudged her hips up towards him, silently encouraging him. A sheen of light sweat covered their bodies. Slowly, so slowly, he started to enter her. Jane felt no pain. Her body seemed to recognise him and welcomed him in deeper and deeper.

'Oh…that feels so good.'

Was that low, husky voice hers?

When he drew out again she whimpered, until he thrust back in all the way. She wrapped her legs around his back, as if to draw him in even deeper, tighter. His strokes were long and hard and assured. She felt the anticipation build once again. After what seemed like an eternity of sensation, building and building until she thought she'd expire, his pace quickened and his movements became less controlled, as if he couldn't hold on. And she couldn't either.

She felt herself tense. Xavier was thrusting so deep that she bit her lips to stop from crying out at the exquisite pleasure of it... And then she came, fast and strong, only dimly registering Xavier's final thrust as his whole body went taut and she felt his own orgasm deep inside her.

They lay locked together for some time. Xavier shifted slightly so that his heavy weight was off her, his hand drifting idly up and down her back. Jane couldn't help a feeling of serene completion from stealing over her. As if she was now whole. He was still part of her, hadn't pulled away yet from her body's tight embrace.

He opened his eyes, that brilliant green pinning her to the spot.

'Are you OK?'

She nodded her head, incapable of speech, her eyes drawn helplessly to his. They lay face to face, her hands captured against his chest, his arms around her. She was mesmerised by every part of him—his eyes, nose, mouth. She reached a finger up to trace his lips wonderingly. He gently pulled himself from her body and she blushed.

He shook his head wryly. 'You're the first virgin I've slept with since my teens...I suspected, but wasn't sure, and when you didn't say anything—'

Jane coloured, wanting to hide. Her virginity had been the last thing on her mind.

'If I'd known...'

She felt herself tense slightly. 'If...if you'd known, what?'

He wouldn't have pursued her? He preferred his women more experienced?

His hand drifted up and down her back, relaxing her again. 'It doesn't matter now. To think I'm your first lover is actually the most erotic thing I've experienced in...'

He didn't finish, just bent and kissed her mouth with aching tenderness. What had she expected after all? The man was sinfully gorgeous, powerful and rich. Of course he was experienced, used to women falling at his feet. She locked her misgivings away somewhere deep inside her.

He curled her into him more tightly, and finally she drifted off to sleep, enclosed in his arms, his strong heart beating under her cheek.

Jane woke the next morning to face an expanse of naked chest. Lifted her eyes slowly to meet green ones looking back. A heavy, possessive arm lay across her hip, the hand moving in slow circles.

'Morning,' she said shyly, wanting to duck her head as the previous night came back into her consciousness. She felt a pleasurable ache in every muscle.

'Morning.' He pressed a kiss to her mouth.

She could feel some tension in the air, and his eyes took on a serious light, making a finger of something skate up and down her spine.

'I didn't use protection last night. I never usually forget, but…' A strange expression came over his face, but it was bland again in a second, making her think she'd imagined it.

'I'm guessing you're probably not on the Pill?'

Reality crashed in on Jane, waking her sleep-muddled brain up in a second. Of course he wouldn't want any complications from this…holiday fling. Because that was all it was. She tried to remain unaware of his naked body stretched close against hers, where she could already feel the stirrings of his arousal, and felt herself responding, with heat unfurling in her lower body. She struggled to focus on his words, not the response of her body.

'No, I'm not…but it's a safe time of the month for me…'

It wasn't strictly accurate, but she did a quick calculation in her head. She was sure it would be fine. Seemingly content with her assurance, he relaxed and drew her in tighter against his body, where she could feel the full strength of his hardness as it pressed against her.

'I think you owe me at least a day in bed…to make up for making me wait…'

All previous thoughts fled as her pulse threatened to strangle her words. She was already breathing faster as his hand caressed the globe of her bottom. 'You knew better than me…you must have known the torture I was going through.'

'No…I was going through my own… In fact it's happening again—something you can help me remedy…'

He drew her on top of him, running his hands down her smooth back, cupping her bottom, bringing up her legs to either side of him. He drew her head down to his, and as she closed her eyes she thought that she'd never get enough of him.

Over the next two days they made love, talked, ate. Xavier revelled in teaching her how much her body could respond to his touch…and how he could respond to hers.

Jane shut out the outside world. Even when they went beyond the confines of the castle and he took her on a sightseeing tour of the rest of the island, it felt as though the island itself was the perimeter of this world, that nothing could intrude. He brought her to the small village, with exactly two hundred and seven inhabitants. It was a bustling, thriving community—largely thanks to him. The people considered themselves markedly different from the mainland, with their Spanish heritage, and it was reflected everywhere. The locals welcomed him as if he was their king…the children shy, men respectful, young women blushing.

Jane knew that without his presence there was no way the island would have retained its unique heritage.

Xavier had promised to show her his favourite childhood spot for swimming, and as they drove there another Jeep approached them on the small narrow road. When it drew alongside the driver was gesturing. Xavier stopped and got out. Jane followed. A stunning brunette, clad in an exquisite suit, was embracing Xavier energetically, speaking fast and furiously.

Jane walked around to join them, feeling very mussed-up and plain next to this vision of chic. Xavier pulled her close and cut through the other woman's stream of words. 'Sophie Vercors…meet Jane Vaughan.'

The woman halted with comic surprise as Jane was revealed, her eyes widening, and then a mischievous look dawned, an undeniable warmth in her face.

She replied in English, 'Xavier, you dark horse…entertaining on the island? Why, I thought you never—'

He cut her off with a warning look in his eye. 'Sophie, Jane is on holiday from England. She goes home in two days.'

Jane felt the brusque comment like a physical slap. He was very tacitly stating the extent of their involvement…

She held out a hand and smiled, ignoring an ache somewhere deep inside. 'Nice to meet you.'

'You too, Jane.' Sophie's smile was wide and unaffected. She had obviously decided to drop any further probing, and launched into a long and hilarious explanation of how she had to race to the mainland to meet her husband, who had forgotten something. She left after a few minutes with a friendly wink to Jane, a flurry of kisses and a cloud of dust in her wake.

Xavier didn't elaborate, beyond telling Jane that she was a Parisienne who had married one of his oldest friends. He, like Xavier, worked primarily on the mainland. It was obvious that she and Xavier were very good friends, easily affectionate with each other.

After a short drive, they pulled in off the track and made their way on foot to the secluded cove. They left the picnic Jane had prepared under a tree on the edge of the beach and raced each other into the water. All thoughts of the future, and her looming departure, were gone, and Jane strenuously focused on the present moment.

In the water, their horseplay quickly turned into something more serious, and afterwards, under the shade of the tree,

Xavier laid out the blanket and stood before her. Hair slicked against his head, the tang of the salty water on his skin, Xavier removed her bikini, kissing every exposed piece of flesh until he came to kneel before her. Her hands were on his shoulders, and her legs were threatening to buckle under waves of intense pleasure as he held her bottom. He wouldn't allow her to fall as his mouth and tongue did wicked things between her legs. Finally, when she thought she couldn't bear it any more, with words pleading for release on her lips, he laid her down and stretched over her, his body long and lean, every muscle clearly delineated, his erection jutting proudly, majestically between their bodies.

Jane felt a primal possessiveness as she looked into his eyes. *This man is mine...*

And it scared her to death. She drove it away, reaching up, her lips seeking and finding his, saying his name on a moan. 'Xavier...now, please now.'

'What...what do you want?'

She urged her hips to his, but he went with her, thwarting her efforts. She bit her lip in frustration.

He took a second to slip on protection, and the knowledge that he hadn't failed to do so since that first time was all too clear in Jane's head. But the throbbing of her body drowned that thought out as she felt him position himself between her legs in one fluid move.

'Tell me what you want...is it this?'

He started to enter the heart of her, just with the tip, and pulled out again.

Jane was nearly mindless with need, barely coherent. 'Yes...yes! Please, Xavier, I can't...hold on...'

He continued to torture her, focusing his attention on her breasts, taking each peak with a hot mouth and stimulating them unbearably, and then his mouth found hers, tongue stroking hers, igniting an ever-climbing fire of need that raced along every vein and cell.

Finally he entered her again, a little deeper, but this time Jane wanted to frustrate *him* and she pulled back. Much as it pained her, it excited her unbearably, this erotic dance.

'Two can play that game…' she breathed with a new confidence.

'Oh, really…?' Xavier growled low in his throat. 'We'll see about that.'

He cupped her bottom, tilting it upwards, laying her bare to his gaze, not allowing her to move, and with one deep thrust entered her so completely that she cried out with pleasure. He didn't allow her any quarter as he drove in and out with a relentless rhythm, sometimes shallow, sometimes deep, until at last they tipped over the precipice of extreme pleasure together, and down into a state of such bliss that it was some time before either one could move.

For the rest of the afternoon, as the light fell, they ate and watched the sun set over the horizon. Jane couldn't help but feel that this was possibly the happiest she had ever been in her life, and she tried to keep it from her eyes, fearing it must be blatantly obvious every time he looked at her.

The next morning she woke in the bed to find Xavier already up. She rolled over onto her side and tucked her head into her arm. Her last day on the island.

With a heavy heart she got up and dressed. She went downstairs and found him in the kitchen, sipping from a cup of coffee. She tried to project a light front, when inside she felt as though she was shrivelling up.

He looked up, a dazzling smile illuminating his face when he saw her in the doorway.

'I have to go to the mainland for a couple of hours today…you could stay here, or come with me if you like?'

Jane poured herself a cup of coffee, praying that he wouldn't notice the tremor in her hands. Delay the inevitable? One more night? Was is so self-indulgent to want to hang on to the fantasy?

A rogue dark part of her answered, 'I'll stay here, if you don't mind…'

He frowned for a second. 'When did you say your flight was?'

'Tomorrow night…I'll have to get back to the villa first thing in the morning, to clean it up and make sure everything is tidied away…pack my things.'

He thought for a second. 'Well, look, why don't you come back to the mainland with me today? You can do your things at the villa, pack and lock it up while I'm busy, and then we could spend the night at the hotel. You could leave from there tomorrow.'

Her heart twisted at his matter-of-fact tone. He was obviously having no qualms at the thought of her leaving. She had an irrational fear that once they stepped off the island, all this would fade as if it never happened.

But what he was saying made perfect sense. Perfect practical sense. He wouldn't understand if she said she'd prefer their last night to be here…to hang on to the dream for as long as possible. No, it was for the best. The break would be easier surrounded by the hustle and bustle of the real world.

Maybe he wanted them to be surrounded by people, the town, in case she became clingy, refused to go. Was he used to women acting that way? She wouldn't be one of those women—couldn't have him suspect for a moment how deeply involved she'd become.

'Yes…yes, of course you're right…'

CHAPTER SIX

AN HOUR later, bag packed and ready to go, Jane waited by the front entrance of the castle. She turned around and drank in the view, committing it all to memory, sucked in the air deeply. The morning sun was gathering more and more heat. In late June its potency was powerful, and the distinctive smell of sun-baked earth wafted over her. The cicadas' incessant chatter stopped, and then started further away every time she moved to try and catch them out.

In the space of just one week she had come to really love this island. That first forbidding view had hidden something much more complex. It had a heart and a vitality that was artfully disguised by its appearance. Completely unique. Much like the man who was striding through the doors towards her now. Every line of his physique screamed dynamic…independent…successful. He reminded her of a lone wolf. Who would get to tame him in the end? Could any one woman do it?

She schooled her features as he approached, and let him take her bag to swing it into the back of his car, which would take them to the boat.

As they got close to the private marina at the harbour on the mainland, Jane could see someone waiting for them. It was the beautiful blonde woman she had noticed that first time she had seen him in the street.

She was waving gaily as the boat approached, but Jane could see her arm falter slightly when she noticed Xavier had a companion.

As they climbed out Jane took Xavier's helping hand, a familiar tingle travelling up her arm, slightly breathless when she came to stand beside him. The other woman didn't even glance Jane's way as she unleashed a torrent of French at Xavier. She was stunning, her perfectly proportioned petite figure and deep tan set off by white jeans and a tight white shirt, artfully tousled blonde hair cascaded down her back.

Xavier drew Jane in to his side with a possessive arm, and when he could get a word in edgeways interjected in English. 'Sasha, don't be so rude. I'd like you to meet Jane. She's been my guest for the past week. You haven't been able to get me because I made sure I was unavailable. Jane, this is Sasha—one of my assistants.'

His tone, while light, held a steely undertone. Jane shivered, and felt a little sorry for Sasha. Any hint of which was swiftly gone when the girl turned her exacting gaze on Jane. Pure venom. She sneaked a look at Xavier, to see if he had noticed, but he had let go of her to rope off the boat, and had moved away a few feet. Jane was acutely conscious of her added inches and bigger frame as the woman sent a scathing glance up and down, summarily dismissing her. Her accent when she spoke was captivating, her English impeccable.

'So nice to meet you…thank you for entertaining Xavi for me…he works far too hard. Tell me, England, is it? You're a tourist?'

Jane nodded warily, feeling hackles that she'd never known she possessed rise.

'Ah, I thought so… Xavi is incorrigible—such a weakness for the—'

But whatever she'd been going to say was halted when Xavier came back to stand beside them.

'Jane, I'll give you a lift to the villa. Sasha, will you arrange for a car to pick Jane up this afternoon? Say around four p.m.'

Jane was still slightly stunned from Sasha's words, not sure where she had been going and not sure if she wanted to know. She looked at her uneasily. Her beautiful smile didn't go near her chocolate-brown eyes. Jane didn't want anything to do with this woman, and remembered belatedly with relief, 'I still have my hire car. I have to get it back anyway, so I'll make my own way to the hotel later.'

These words earned positive waves of radioactivity from the other woman. Jane avoided her eye, relieved when Xavier said, 'Fine. Sasha, I'll see you in the office in about an hour.'

Back in the villa, after Xavier had dropped her off, Jane wandered around disconsolately. She went through the motions of cleaning up and packing. She felt as though she were empty inside, and tried to shake the feeling off.

She made a light lunch for herself, and carried it up to the terrace, remembering back to the night she had stood there, dreaming about him—the night after she had bumped into him in the street. Wandering back to take in the view, she had to smile a little sad smile to herself.

Well, her fantasy had come true. Spectacularly. It had come to life...*he* had come to life...brought *her* to life in ways she would have never envisaged. He had awakened her. Been her first lover. Opened her eyes to a sensuality she had never imagined herself to possess. Helped her to own that sensuality. He had been her gift for the past week...and tonight would be their last night.

She would have to let him go. Be strong. She wouldn't fall at his feet, weeping and wailing. He belonged in this world of unimaginable wealth and beauty. Every day blessed by the benediction of the sun. And she belonged... She didn't belong here.

God knew what it was that attracted him to her...but he

was offering her one more night. And she would take it. Savour it. And somehow find the strength to walk away tomorrow with her head held high.

Later, when Jane walked into the hotel lobby after dropping the car off, she felt a little more in control of her emotions. Xavier had told her to give her name to the receptionist, who would be expecting her. She did so, and a bellboy came to take her luggage and show her up to the penthouse suite.

When she got up there she couldn't see any sign of him, and her heart slowed to a regular beat again. She spied a bottle of champagne in an ice bucket, with a note and pristine white rose resting against its side. With trembling fingers she opened the note after smelling the rose. The handwriting was big and curt. She smiled, imagining his impatience.

I'm sorry I'm not here to meet you. Have a glass of champagne while you are waited on hand and foot, and I will be there to pick you up at 7.30. *A bientôt.* X

For a minute she wondered if the X meant a kiss or was just his initial, before trying to figure out the rest of the message. A knock came and she went to answer it, still puzzling over his note.

At the door were three women, all carrying various accoutrements. The light dawned when they came in and told Jane they were there to do a massage, pedicure, manicure, facial, her hair...in no special order. Her mouth dropped open, but they were too well trained to make any comment when it became apparent that they were dealing with a novice. Having never indulged herself like this before, Jane, after a moment of trepidation and the old haunting guilt, gave herself over to the experience. And went to heaven and back.

A couple of hours later, when they'd left, she went to one of the mirrors and stared incredulously. Another creature looked back. A relaxed, buffed, shining version of herself, with sleek hair that fell in a smooth wave to just below her jaw. They had tinted her eyelashes, which she had never had done before, and now her eyes seemed huge in her face, framed by thick luxurious lashes.

Before she could lose herself in uncustomary narcissistic bliss, she spied the clock out of the corner of her eye and saw that it was almost seven-fifteen. In a panic, she realised that she hadn't even unpacked—and what could she possibly wear that he hadn't already seen by now? With dismay, she pulled her bag into the bedroom and stopped when she saw the bed. A huge white box lay there, with another note and a red rose this time.

Just in case. X

She opened the box with clumsy fingers and pulled out a dress from the folds of tissue paper. And what a dress. It slid through her fingers when she tried to hold it. She gathered it back again, and stared in shock. It screamed *designer*. Sure enough, the label confirmed her suspicion. She mightn't be a fount of knowledge when it came to celebrity and celebrity lifestyles, but even she recognised the famous name. It must be worth a fortune. She spied more in the box, and opened up the paper to reveal a matching set of silk and lace underwear. Silk stockings. Even shoes.

Against every penny-scrimping sensibility that had been drummed into her, she couldn't resist. She allowed the hotel robe to drop from her shoulders and she pulled on the underwear before stepping into the dress. It was strapless and tight-fitting. She looked at herself in the mirror. Was it meant to cling like that? Especially around her breasts? She looked behind...her bottom looked so...round.

She heard the door and her heart thudded to a stop, before starting up again at twice the speed.

'Jane? Where are you?'

'In…in here… Wait! I'll come out.'

She felt suddenly panicked at the thought of him coming into the bedroom. With a deep breath, and squaring her shoulders, she opened the door and went into the suite.

Xavier was pouring himself a glass of champagne, and he looked up, his hand stilling in the action. He put the bottle down slowly as his gaze raked her up and down from under his lashes. He had to put his hands into his pockets in a reflex action, to stop himself from reaching out and hauling her against his chest and crushing that soft kissable mouth under his.

She looked…stunning. The dress showed off her figure to perfection, emphasising her hourglass shape, exactly as he had imagined. And her eyes… Lord, those eyes…with their innocently sensual promise—they made him want to lock all the doors, take her and bury himself so deep inside her that she'd never want another man again.

He shook himself mentally. It was a nice dress. No need to go over the top about it. He'd seen plenty of women in far more revealing dresses. Taken them off too. And he would again in the future. Jane Vaughan was going home tomorrow, and it was a good thing… He'd been far too uncomfortably aware of alien emotions all week. Time to say goodbye and get back to normal. He had one more night. To get her out of his system for good.

He dropped heavy lids over his eyes and bent to pour another glass of champagne before strolling over and passing it to her.

Jane still hadn't moved—had been rendered immobile under his very thorough inspection. She covered up her insecurity by taking a gulp of the sparkling vintage wine. The bubbles made her nose screw up, and she immediately felt silly for worrying. She was going to enjoy this last night, be free and easy.

Xavier said throatily, 'To you…you look beautiful tonight.'

'Thank you…so do you.' And he did. Darkly handsome in a black tuxedo. The snowy white shirt making his eyes stand out, that glittering phenomenal green.

'Thank you for…laying on the massage and things today and this…' She indicated the dress shyly.

'My pleasure…' And it would be, later, he vowed, struck again by her charming politeness. He was used to women expecting…taking from him. 'I've booked a restaurant on the seafront for dinner…it's not far. We can stroll, if you think you can in those shoes.'

'I'll be fine…' Jane vowed that even if her feet were bleeding she wouldn't say a word; she didn't want a moment of the evening to be spoiled.

He took her glass, and they were almost at the door when she stopped in her tracks by his side in sudden embarrassment.

'I didn't put any make-up on… I can't go out in a dress like this with no—'

Xavier put a finger to her lips, silencing her. He looked at her carefully and came very close, one hand on either side of her face. Then he bent his head and brought his mouth to hers and kissed her.

Taken aback slightly for a second, Jane quickly forgot everything—where they were, where they were going—as the kiss deepened, and she brought her hands up to steady herself on his chest, the beat of his heart starting up a throbbing in her own pulse. With masterful expertise Xavier plumbed the depths of her mouth, and then, achingly slowly, traced her lips with his tongue before delving back in and stoking a fire that had heat travel from the molten centre of her all the way up to where she could feel her breasts aching heavily against their confinement.

He lifted his head, breathing harshly. Jane opened her eyes reluctantly. He saw her cheeks flushed with a burgeoning arousal, her eyes glittering like stars under long black spiky lashes, and her lips… He almost kicked the door closed behind him, painfully aware of his own arousal… Her lips were full and swollen and moist, like two crushed petals.

'There…' he said gruffly. 'You don't need any make-up.'

Taking her hand firmly in his, he pulled her behind him. Jane stumbled to keep up, bringing a hand up to sensitised lips. What did he mean by that?

When she caught her reflection in the elevator mirror a few seconds later she saw exactly what he had meant, and blushed from her toes to the tip of her head.

The restaurant was exclusive. When they arrived the bouncers fell over themselves to be the one to admit Xavier and his guest. The maître d' fawned and fussed as he led them to a table tucked away from the main floor by an open window. Strategically placed plants ensured the kind of privacy that allowed them to see the rest of the room and yet not be observed themselves. A white tablecloth, sparkling silverware, gleaming glasses. Candlelight. Jane sighed and smiled. She couldn't have done better if she had actually written it down on paper.

'What's so amusing?'

She looked at him across the table, so at ease in these surroundings, supremely confident. He would never understand where she was from…where she had to go back to. How special this was for her.

She shrugged lightly. 'Nothing…I'm enjoying the spectacle of all the minions tripping over themselves to impress you.'

'But not you, Jane…you didn't trip over yourself to impress me. You're different.'

Different… Which made reference to all those other women…

A short, sharp dart arrowed its way into her heart. She spoke lightly to disguise it.

'Well…my cunning plan worked, didn't it?'

'Ah…as I thought. You're as mercenary as the rest of them…'

See?

'Yes…' A brittle laugh came out of somewhere. 'You see, I've actually been stalking you for months, and I devised the best, most effective way to get your attention.'

'I thought you looked familiar in the street that day.'

He wagged a triumphant finger at her. Even though they were joking, she felt sad. Though he hadn't let it appear too often, she knew he harboured a well-worn cynicism.

The waiter appeared and took their order. Jane pushed aside all reservations, judgements, fears, and focused entirely on the moment—and Xavier. All too effortlessly she succeeded, and the conversation flowed like a burbling stream. Joyfully, easily, and far, far too seductively to resist.

She barely noticed the courses being delivered. She must have eaten, but for the life of her she couldn't remember what. She found herself watching him talk, committing every part of his hard-boned face to memory. The way his eyes crinkled ever so slightly when he smiled, the glimpse of bright white teeth. The way he inclined his head, encouraging her to go on when she faltered during a story.

All too soon it was time to go. The last drops of wine had been drunk, the espresso cups were taken away. A bare tablecloth sat between them. Xavier stood easily and held out a hand. She allowed him to pull her up, a little unsteady with the effects of the wine. He slipped an arm around her waist and together they walked out. His scent was heavy and potent in her nostrils. She had to stop herself from turning into his chest and breathing deeply.

Instead of going back the way they had come, he led her down by the beach. She hesitated for a second, before taking off her shoes and then reaching up under her dress to pull down her stockings.

'Wait.'

Her hands stilled as Xavier crouched down in front of her.

They were sheltered from the main promenade by a tree, the sound of the sea only feet way.

'Let me.'

Jane stood and closed her eyes as she felt his hands come up under her dress to encircle one thigh, fingers stalling, and slowly snagging the stocking top to bring it down. Exquisite pleasure. Especially when his hands seemed to take far too long to travel their way up her other leg. She was shaking, her hands heavy on his shoulders by the time he reached his destination and pulled the other stocking down, trembling with the unbearable desire for him to keep going up…fingers reaching higher until they found…

He stood up lithely, dangling her shoes and stockings with one hand. On impulse she reached up and tugged at his bow tie until it came loose and free, then undid his top button, tongue between her teeth when it proved stiff and unwieldy.

When she had finished she looked up to find him staring down at her, eyes fixated on her mouth. She innocently moistened her lips with her tongue.

He took her hand with urgency, and led her onto the beach. 'There's a quick way back to the hotel from here…'

Jane barely took in the magical view as they made their silent way across the beach, the moonlight bathing everything with a milky glow, sounds of laughter and muted music coming from the strip on the other side of the bushes.

Soon they were at the steps that led up to the gardens at the back of the hotel. They stood there looking at each other, lost in the moment. Then he handed her the shoes and stockings and disappeared—before she felt an arm coming under her legs and herself being lifted and held against his broad chest.

'Xavier…you can't.'

'There's gravel on the ground up here, and I can't wait for you to put your shoes on… As sexy as you are walking in them, it'll take too long…'

'Too long for what?'

'To get you where I want you…on my bed…under me.'

She buried her head in his shoulder as they approached the hotel, arms around his neck. She felt extraordinarily cherished and protected and desired. They avoided bumping into anyone, and took the service elevator all the way up, coming in to the penthouse from another entrance. He didn't put her down until they reached the bedroom.

Shoes and stockings fell from nerveless fingers as he slowly lowered her down his body. When her feet touched the floor they were standing so close that she could feel his heart beating against her chest.

In what felt like slow motion, her zip was pulled down, buttons popped open, catches undone. There was the whisper of clothes falling to the floor, skin meeting skin, soft and hard and silky, tongues touching and tasting, legs buckling, falling onto the bed in a tangle of limbs. Jane shut her eyes and ears to the voices in her head, concentrating on Xavier's hand as it glided over her breasts and down across her belly, down further…

When Jane woke the next morning she was alone in the bed. Just then the bathroom door opened and Xavier emerged, with an indecently small towel around his waist. She felt a blush coming on when she remembered the previous night… To think of how wanton she'd been…had become in the space of a few days. Where on earth had she ever got the nerve to do those things to him?

He watched the expressions flit over her face. Did she have any idea how beguiling she looked? How much it turned him on to think that he was the only lover she'd ever known? She looked at him, sleepy eyes, flushed cheeks, biting her lip, pulling the sheet up. He strode over to the bed and came down on his arms beside her. Her eyes widened, the pupils dilating. It firmed his resolve for what he was going to ask her. But not yet. Later. He pressed a quick kiss to her lips and straightened.

'Morning, sleepy. I'm sorry about this, but there's an emergency with the hotel in Malaysia and I have a crisis meeting to attend… Stay put, and I'll be right back. We can have breakfast together.'

'OK…'

Jane watched dry-mouthed as he let the towel drop and unselfconsciously pulled on his clothes. What a body.

When she heard the main door close she rolled over, burying her face in the pillow. She had to face it. Couldn't block it out any more. Especially after last night. He had brought her to the height of something so beautiful that she knew without a doubt that she would never experience anything remotely close with another man.

She had fallen in love with him. Hard and deep and fast. Irrevocably. Unbelievably. Needless to say he had made no indication that to him this was anything more than a brief diversion, which was ending today. She wouldn't allow her thoughts to fly ahead a few hours, when she would have to think about leaving. As if ignoring it would make it less of a reality.

Forcing herself to block the dangerous thoughts, telling herself she had to be crazy, she got up and went to have a quick shower, noticing faint marks on her body and colouring when she remembered herself urging Xavier to go harder, how she had assured him that he didn't need to be so gentle. She groaned under the powerful jet of water.

After towelling her hair and donning a voluminous robe, she wandered into the suite and opened the windows, looking out over the pool area and the sea beyond, breathing in the warm morning air.

There was a knock on the door. That was funny—didn't he have a key? Jane went and opened the door, a ready smile on her lips.

'Missing me already?'

CHAPTER SEVEN

HER smile faded fast when she saw who it was at the door. Sasha.

His assistant looked sparkly and bright. As if she'd been up for hours. Before Jane knew what was happening, Sasha had sidled past her and into the room, looking around with interest.

'If you're looking for Xavier, he's gone for a meeting—'

She turned and fixed Jane with cold eyes. 'I know *exactly* where he is. I *always* know where he is.'

'I'll tell him you called…' Jane stayed by the open door and hoped she would take the hint.

'Actually, I came to see you.'

Sasha sat on the couch, crossing one elegant leg over the other. Where was this going?

'Did you enjoy last night? The pampering….the restaurant?'

How did she know about that? Jane felt a stillness come into her body, as if it were preparing for some kind of attack. Her hand gripped the knob of the door.

'Yes, thank you,' she said faintly, dimly thinking to herself, Well, maybe she booked it for him, so she'd be bound to know…

'Oh, yes! I nearly forgot about the champagne and everything else…'

A dull roaring sensation was beginning somewhere in her head as Sasha continued.

'I hope I organised it all to Xavier's satisfaction. I thought I'd check with you to make sure I did a good job…'

'You…you organised everything?'

She knows about the dress?

Sasha threw back her head and laughed. 'Of course, silly! You don't think someone like Xavier has time to go around booking restaurants and making facial appointments do you?'

Jane's brain was barely taking in her words any more.

And the notes? Surely not those…

Holding onto the door as if it were a lifeline, she fought for composure. 'Sasha, why don't you say what you want to say and get out…I have to pack.'

'I wouldn't be doing my job if I didn't make sure that *all* of Xavi's women were looked after.'

She stood up and sauntered close to Jane, who held her breath, just wanting the other woman gone.

'I have to admit, it gets a bit boring after a while. I keep telling him not to be so predictable, to vary things a bit…' Sasha smiled indulgently. 'But I guess he's just old-fashioned. That's why I'm here, Jane. I can see the type of woman you are. You're not like the others.' She looked at Jane closely before a cruel smile twisted her lips, 'You've fallen for him haven't you?'

Jane said nothing. Couldn't move a muscle.

'You poor thing… It'll be someone else next week, you know…the same thing all over again. Like I said, you seem nice, and I'd hate to see you get hurt. He hates clingy women. *Au revoir.*'

And just like that she sashayed out of the room.

Jane felt as though she'd been punched in the stomach. She actually couldn't suck enough air into her belly for a minute, and had to take calming breaths to prevent working herself into a panic attack. She stumbled over to the mini-bar and pulled out a bottle of water, taking a deep gulp. She felt shivery and nauseous. She sat down on a chair and stared blindly in front of her.

Stupid, stupid Jane. Allowing herself to fall in love with him. If Sasha had picked up on it, then who was to say he hadn't either? Utter humiliation rose up and swamped her. Words that Sasha had said dropped like stones into Jane's numbed brain: *So predictable...someone else next week...all of Xavi's women...*

She stood suddenly. Well, she wouldn't be waiting here for him like a lame duck. She tripped over the robe in her haste to get into the bedroom, and packed quickly and feverishly, throwing on trousers and a shirt, uncaring if they matched or not. The dress lay on the floor, where it had landed last night, a cruel reminder. She didn't bother to call for a bellboy in case they alerted Xavier.

She was outside the hotel and hailing a cab, sitting in it with the driver looking at her expectantly before she could function. She still had hours to go before her plane that night. She directed him to the villa. It was the only other place she could think of. She'd wait there until she had to leave.

Up in the villa, she felt as though she could breathe again. Despite all her brave ideas, notions, how had she ever thought she could walk away unscathed? Sasha hadn't told her anything she hadn't suspected on some level, she had just pointed out the truth...showed her the proof, so to speak. And it hurt like hell. But better that it hurt now. Better than if she'd been waiting in the suite for him to come back. Better than if he'd seen something in her eyes. She could well imagine the panicked look that might have crossed his face, the pity in his eyes as he gently had to tell her that it had been fun...but it was over. No, Sasha had done her a favour.

She heard the low rumble of an engine, which got louder before finally stopping outside the front door. She jumped up. The unmistakable sound of a door being slammed came, and a large shape appeared on the other side of the front door, a harsh knock on the glass.

'Jane! Jane, are you in there? Open this door now. I know you're there…'

Xavier.

She stood behind the wall for a moment, her heart thudding so loudly and heavily that she felt a little faint. The nausea was returning with a vengeance.

She went on shaky limbs to open the door, pasting what she hoped was a bland smile on her face.

He stood there bristling, dark glasses covering his eyes, hands on hips.

'Xavier…'

He pushed his glasses onto his head, and with the sun behind him Jane was blinded for a moment. He took advantage and walked into the open-plan hall. Jane stayed by the door.

'Well? Are you always this rude, or is it just with me?' he asked with deceptive calm.

Every line in her body screamed from being held so tightly. 'What's the big deal, Xavier? I wanted to come back here to collect some things I'd forgotten, and was hoping to get to say goodbye before leaving…'

He came and stood far too close. 'Liar. You were planning on leaving. Sasha told me.'

'What?'

'When I went back to the room and you were gone, I went looking for you. I met Sasha in the lobby and she told me she'd just seen you get in a cab—said you'd told her that you were leaving.'

'But she—' She stopped. What could she say? That Sasha had told her exactly how it was…what his little routine was…how she had organised everything, made it all too easy for his holiday *fling*?

She would not humiliate herself.

'Well?' he asked softly.

Jane wasn't sure what Sasha was playing at. Maybe she

wanted him for herself…maybe she already had him… The thought made Jane feel sick again… Maybe she was tired of accommodating his long line of women. But what did it matter anyway? It didn't change the fact that he would be entertaining someone new next week. Why didn't he just let her go? She looked up into his eyes and felt her equilibrium falter, tried to remember his question. Looked away.

'Nothing, Xavier… Look, I have to leave in a few hours, so what's the point? We're never going to see each other again.'

His hand reached out and caught her under her chin, forcing her face to his. The warmth of his fingers made her want to lean into him. She clenched her jaw.

'I wanted to talk to you about that.'

'What…?' She was having trouble concentrating on what he was saying.

'Never seeing each other again… Forget about this morning. Why don't you stay on for a while? You said yourself you're subbing at the moment, without a permanent teaching position. You're free to do what you want.'

The confusion showed in her eyes as she gazed up into his. She hadn't expected this. Her mind, trying to make sense of what he was saying, seized on the banal.

'But…but I can't just stay here… I've got a mortgage…bills to pay.'

'I could take care of all of that,' he dismissed arrogantly.

The treacherous wings of something that had taken off in her heart were fast crumbling. Jane reached up and brought his hand down. 'So…effectively you would pay for me to stay here?'

He shrugged. 'Yes. I could make it easy for you.'

Jane tried to make sense of it.

'You would keep me here as some sort of…paid woman…a mistress? For an affair?'

'Well, it wouldn't be exactly like that.' His hand sliced the air impatiently. 'You make it sound almost sordid.'

He took her hand and lifted it, not letting her pull away. One thumb rotated in her palm, making slow circles. She could feel herself responding. Her body and head going in completely opposite directions.

'Jane…I haven't had enough of you yet…and I know you feel the same way. Stay…for as long as this lasts.'

For as long as this lasts… That was the problem. It wouldn't last for ever for him, and when it was over he'd move on, desire sated and she knew she'd be feeling about a million times worse than this very moment. *He's used to doing this.*

Jane pulled her hand out of his with a jerky movement. The nausea that had diminished rose again, making her feel light-headed, and dirty, tainted, when she thought of how Sasha had set up last night's date for him, as if Jane were some kind of concubine. It lent a harsh quality to her voice.

'No, Xavier. I don't want to be your mistress. You'll find a replacement soon enough. This week has been more than enough for me.'

She'd had enough? Who was she kidding? She'd never get enough of this man. A lifetime wouldn't be enough…and anything less wouldn't do. And he was not in the market for lifetime commitments. How could she have forgotten that first night by the pool? Sherry had told her about his reputation.

She could see the muscle twitch in his jaw, knew she'd made a hit. She held herself erect. His ego might be wounded, but that would be it. He'd get over it. She, on the other hand…wouldn't.

'I'm not interested,' she said, as if to drive the point home.

He took a step back and Jane felt a rush of air between them and a wave of desolation washed over her. The shuttered look descended. A look she hadn't seen since that first time they'd spoken. It made her want to reach out and touch him. He backed away again and put on his shades.

'If that's what you want.'

She nodded miserably, trying to maintain a look of bland indifference. He turned and went through the door.

And then he was gone. The engine gunned fiercely, and with a spurt of gravel it died away into the distance. Jane couldn't keep it down any longer, and just made it to the toilet—where she threw up violently.

Xavier forced his hands to relax their death grip on the wheel as he sped away. What a fool he'd been, allowing her to get under his skin so easily. How dared she turn him down? His hand slapped the wheel. She thought she was too good for him.

An utter fool. That was what he was. She was nothing but a tourist, looking for a story to bring home. The sooner he put the last week and her out of his mind for good, the better.

CHAPTER EIGHT

Nearly Four Months Later

JANE shouldered her way through the door of her one-bedroom ground-floor flat, shutting out the noise of the traffic and wailing sirens. She was soaked. Autumn was here with a vengeance. She dropped the bags of shopping and kicked off her shoes with relief, taking off her layers and leaving them to drip dry in the bathroom. She ran a quick hot bath and afterwards wrapped herself in her dressing gown, feeling a little better. She would have to be more careful. She sat gratefully on her sofa, placing a hand on her belly. She still couldn't believe she was pregnant. But she was.

She remembered the shock of that day when, after weeks of relentless nausea on her return from France and then no sign of her period, dread had settled in her heart. Finally, one day after work, she had worked up the nerve to buy an over the counter test. A positive result. Confirmed by the doctor.

She hadn't told anyone yet. Not even her mother. Even now she was barely able to contain her heartbreak. It was far, far worse than she had imagined. She had fobbed Lisa off when asked about the holiday, being vague, and Lisa thankfully had responded with her usual exasperated roll of the eyes, before launching into the latest adventure of her own love-life.

Her hand moved abstractedly over her belly. She had never contemplated not keeping the baby. That wasn't an option. She sighed heavily as the object of her every waking and sleeping thought intruded.

Xavier.

She knew she couldn't live a lie, couldn't have the baby and not have the truth known. She had to let him know. But how to tell him? How to get in touch with him? How to be prepared in case he got heavy-handed and demanded…what? Jane remembered him telling her that he was last in his line. No doubt an heir figured somewhere in his future. Just not with someone like her.

But would he demand she hand over the baby? She felt a sliver of fear. She didn't think he would be capable, but then he was so powerful. An heir to his fortune was important, necessary for the survival of the island…

She would have to be strong and not let him bully her. She doubted he'd want to be saddled with a small baby anyway. It would seriously cramp his lifestyle.

She grimaced. She'd gone from a world where Xavier had never existed to one in which, since she'd come home, every paper she opened seemed to have a picture of him. In New York, Paris, Milan… In each place a new fortune being made, a new woman on his arm. Each time like a knife in her heart.

She got up wearily and went through the motions of cooking dinner, eating it and tasting nothing. Afterwards she went into the bathroom and saw the pool of water on the floor under her dripping clothes. She went to get the Sunday papers she was about to throw away, opening them out on the floor to soak up the water.

For a second she didn't even notice that she'd stopped breathing, then shook her head as if to clear it. The photo and the words didn't disappear. It was the business section. His face stared at her starkly from the page under a headline:

FRENCH BILLIONAIRE IN UK TO SAVE AILING
HOTEL CHAIN
Xavier Salgado-Lézille, the French entrepreneur, owner
of Lézille island and the exclusive hotel chain of the
same name, is in London this week in negotiations to
save the once luxurious chain of Lancaster hotels...
In recent times they have deteriorated...
Has his own offices in the City...
Other companies interested in his expertise...
Why do we have to look abroad to be saved...?

The words swam up at her from the page. She sank down
oblivious to the wet floor. Checked the date. Yesterday. That
meant he was here this week. Incredibly.

She read it again. He had offices in the City. She went to
her phone book and checked with nerveless fingers. Sure
enough, there it was, the address and phone number. Why
hadn't she thought of that before? She checked the clock. It
was still business hours. Just.

Before she could think or lose her nerve she dialled the
number from the book. A crisp voice answered. She asked to
be put through to Xavier's personal secretary.

'Hello, Molly Parker here.'

'Hello...are you Mr Salgado-Lézille's personal secretary?'

'Yes, I am. May I ask who is calling please?'

'It's...my name is Jane Vaughan. Could you tell him
please that I'd like to make an appointment to see him?'

Her heart was beating so hard and fast she was surprised the
other woman couldn't hear it. Her hands felt slippery with sweat.

His assistant sounded suspicious. 'Very well—please hold
for a moment.'

After a couple of agonising minutes she came back on the
line. 'Mr Salgado will see you at ten-thirty tomorrow
morning. He's very busy, you know—'

'I'm well aware of that. I won't take up much of his time, thank you.'

Jane put down the phone with a shaking hand. Automatically she placed a hand on her belly and sank into the sofa. The phone rang again, shrill in the room. She jumped violently, picking it up warily, as if it would bite her.

'Oh, Mum it's you… No, I wasn't expecting anyone else—don't be silly.'

In the course of the conversation Jane decided it was time to break the news. Now that she was going to see Xavier and tell him. After all, she was beginning to show.

Her mother was disappointed that Jane was going to have the baby on her own, knowing all too well how hard it had been for her after Jane's father died, and she was worried because she and Arthur were going to be leaving England, but Jane made sure to reassure her on that score. The last thing she wanted was to be responsible for Arthur not being able to take his new bride away to their new life. He had grown up in South Africa, and after the honeymoon he had persuaded her mother to emigrate to the warmer climes of Cape Town.

Jane knew her mother was stubborn and that Arthur would do whatever she wanted. They were due to leave in three weeks, and Jane was determined that they go. She hoped she had done the right thing in telling her.

As if the telephone wires were buzzing, the phone rang again shortly after. It was Lisa. She decided to tell her too, feeling a little more weight lift off her shoulders. She refused to say who the father was, only that she was going to see him the next day and that, no, he wouldn't be a part of her life.

After the initial screech Lisa was for once stunned into silence. Jane managed to see the humour and appreciate this uncustomary role-reversal. It was nice to have the support of a friend, but she declined her offer to come with her. She had to face Xavier alone.

* * *

The following morning in the cab, Jane tried to quell the mammoth butterflies in her stomach. She felt nauseous, and knew it wasn't morning sickness. She hadn't had that in a few weeks now. The thought of seeing Xavier again had her blood running cold through her veins. Then hot. How would he look in this climate? Somehow less? As if! She knew all too well that he would stand out like an exotic hothouse flower.

Luckily, after an intensely busy period with work, the teacher she had been subbing for had returned from sick leave, and Jane as yet hadn't been placed anywhere else. She couldn't contemplate it right now.

The cab drew up under an ominously grey sky outside a huge gleaming building.

Salgado-Lézille Enterprises.

After she got out she fought the urge to turn around, step right back into the cab and tell the driver to go back to her flat. Instead she put one foot in front of the other.

Inside the building there was a hushed reverence more in keeping with a cathedral. No doubt because the boss was in attendance, she thought darkly.

At the reception desk she gave her name and got a security tag. Then she was directed to the top floor. The lift was entirely glass, and she could see the ground floor slip away. The panic rose again.

After agonisingly long seconds it came to a stop and the door swished open with a little ping. She stepped into a luxuriously carpeted hall. A pretty girl behind a desk took her name again, and told her where she could wait on a comfortable couch just outside some huge imposing oak doors. Jane had dressed down, in jeans, sneakers and a sweater. She didn't want him to think she was coming here for anything else. And she was protective of her small telltale bump.

The door opened and her heart jumped into her mouth. It

revealed a matronly woman with a neat grey bob. She emerged, holding out a hand.

'Hello, dear, you must be Jane. I'm Molly, Mr Salgado's UK assistant. Please come through.'

Jane stuttered a few words and followed her into an office where Molly took her coat and stopped outside another set of doors. It was like Fort Knox. She rapped lightly on the door, and opened it before turning to let Jane pass through. She felt a hysterical moment of wanting to bury her head in this woman's chest and have her tell her it would all be OK. But she didn't.

When she walked in she couldn't see Xavier at first, the office was so big. She felt at a serious disadvantage. The door clicked shut behind her.

Then she saw him. Standing with hands in his pockets in an exquisite suit before a huge window that took in the whole of London, or so it seemed. His tall dark shape was silhouetted against the skyline. Master of all he surveyed.

The blood rushed to her head and there was a roaring in her ears. He was saying something, coming towards her. She could feel herself swaying for an interminable moment, but just before she fell strong arms came around her and then she was half-sitting, half-lying on some sort of chaise longue. Xavier was crouching down beside her, holding a glass with some dark liquid.

'Here—take a sip of this. You're whiter than a ghost.'

In such close proximity every cell jumped to zinging life. So much for hoping that any attraction might have diminished. It was still there, like a plug going back into a socket. The energy running between them was palpable.

She moved to sit up. 'I'm sorry, I don't know what happened…'

'When was the last time you ate?'

'What?'

'Food—you know, we use it to stay alive. You look as though you haven't eaten a square meal in weeks.'

Jane stifled a defensive retort. She knew she'd lost weight since she'd got home, but she just hadn't had time…and the doctor had reassured her that it was quite a normal phenomenon to actually lose weight when first becoming pregnant.

'I'm fine…it's isn't any concern of yours what I eat or don't eat.'

He left the untouched glass on a table beside her and stepped away. 'Of course not… To what do I owe the pleasure of your visit?'

Jane stood, not liking the way he was towering over her, and was relieved that the dizziness had dissipated somewhat.

'I've come to tell you something.'

His gaze slanted down at her, no trace of warmth on his face.

'Ah…could it be that you're having second thoughts about my offer? Back in the cold, grey reality of England you're realising what an opportunity you passed up?'

She looked at him blankly for a second before exploding, nerves making her reaction stronger. 'Unbelievable…how arrogant is that? You know, I never thought you had such an inflated sense of self, but obviously I was wrong.'

'Well, then, why are you here?' he sneered. 'Hardly to catch up on old times, eh? As I seem recall you were only too eager to see the back of me that morning…couldn't even wait to say goodbye.'

Her head started to pound. This wasn't going to plan. First almost fainting, and now he thought she wanted to be his mistress after all.

'No…I mean yes. Look, I really do have something to tell you, and it's not easy…' She looked at him beseechingly.

She breathed a sigh of relief when she saw him sit down behind his desk. Space. She sat down on the other side, her hands held tight together in her lap.

'The fact is…I know I said that I thought it was OK, but I was wrong…the truth is…'

'Yes?' he bit out impatiently.

She squared her chin and looked at him unflinchingly. 'I'm pregnant.'

The words dropped into a deafening silence. He didn't react. His face was like a mask, Jane had a moment of clarity when she knew that was why he was so successful at business—a perfect poker face. He got up and went to stand at the window with his back to her.

'Xavier...'

'I heard you,' he said, in a curiously flat voice. Then he turned around abruptly, green eyes pinning her to the spot.

'It's mine?' A slight inflection made it a question.

She stood angrily, her whole frame quivering. 'Well, of course it's yours...how dare you imply that you might not be the father? I haven't had time to do anything since I got home much less find a new lover and try to get pregnant in the gleeful anticipation of tracking you down and trying to pass the baby off as yours.'

He ran an impatient hand through his hair, and for the first time she noticed lines on his face that she didn't remember. He looked tired.

'Look, I'm sorry...it's just a bit much to take in. How much...when are you due?'

'In March.'

'It must have been that first time.'

'Yes.' Jane felt a blush ascending from her chest all the way up to her face. Couldn't stop the torrent of images that were all too frequent, haunting her imagination. She tried to avoid his focus. She started babbling. 'Ah...look, I just wanted to let you know. The last thing I want is for you to feel that you have to be responsible for anything...I don't expect anything from you at all. I'm going to bring the baby up myself. Of course you can come and see him...or her...whenever you want. Why don't I let you get used to the idea?'

She placed a card on the table. 'That's my address and number.'

She was practically at the door before he seemed to break himself out of his stupor. 'Jane, wait...we need to talk about this.'

Just then the door opened, and Molly appeared with some men behind her.

'Not now, Molly, please.'

Even Jane balked at the barely leashed anger in his voice, but Molly seemed to have weathered worse, and stood her ground.

'Mr Salgado, it's the men from Tokyo...remember, they only have one hour in London before they have to fly to New York? You yourself specifically requested this meeting.'

Jane took full advantage of the opportunity and fled before he could stop her, grabbing her coat, mumbling a goodbye to Molly.

Xavier tried to keep his mind on the meeting after Jane left but, the truth was that he was blown away. Everything was distilled down to her and the fact that she was pregnant. He still felt remnants of the pure elation that had surged through him when he had seen her again. Then the concern that had ripped through him when she had gone so white and almost collapsed. The feel of her slender body in his arms...his inappropriate response.

Alone again in his office, he held her card in his hand. The truth was that he had been in possession of her address for a couple of months now. It hadn't been hard to trace her. He wasn't sure if he'd really planned on getting in touch with her. But one thing was for certain: he hadn't been able to get her out of his head. Oh, he had tried. With various women. But when it had come to it, he just couldn't. Her face, the smell of her body...the way she had responded to his touch...would flash into his head and render him more or less impotent.

Him...impotent!

He obviously just hadn't had enough of her—needed to get her out of his system once and for all. When he'd heard

she had phoned he had thought it was because she'd realised
the same thing. But it wasn't.

Pregnant. The word fell heavily into his head. It brought
up images, memories… A dark emotion threatened to rise up.
His fists clenched. He wouldn't think about that now. Things
were complicated. However, he knew what he wanted with
a fierceness that surprised him. He didn't want to look too
closely at his reasoning yet, or why it was so strong, he just
knew it was the only solution. And he knew exactly how to
get to her to comply, whether she wanted to or not.
Uncomfortably he was aware that it was more than likely *not*.
And he didn't like how that felt.

That evening Jane tried to relax. It was impossible. Her whole
body felt as though it had received an injection of some vital
life force energy. When she had got back to the flat she'd
changed into tracksuit bottoms and an old baggy sweatshirt.

Xavier was in the country, and as long as he was she
couldn't rest easy. She hoped that he would just leave her
alone. Let her get on with things.

The doorbell rang.

It couldn't be…could it? She went towards the door, her
hands balled into fists, opening it warily.

'Dominic.' She breathed a sigh of relief, but also felt a stab
of disappointment. Lisa's brother stood on the doorstep. She
hadn't seen him since she'd got back, had avoided his per-
sistent calls.

'Come in…what are you doing here?' She ushered him
into the sitting room.

He was shy, as usual, not really able to meet her eye.
'Look, I won't beat around the bush…Lisa told me about
your…being pregnant.'

A blush stained his freckled cheeks, and Jane's heart went
out to him, but she didn't interrupt.

'The thing is, Jane…well, you know how I feel about you.

I came to say that I'm here if you need someone to lean on. That is, if you'd have me, I'd marry you.'

A lump came into her throat. 'Oh, Dominic…that's so sweet. I'm very flattered that you would offer to marry me, but the truth is—'

The doorbell rang again. Jane muttered an apology and went to open it.

Xavier.

Standing on the doorstep, crowding the small doorway.

The breath was driven from her lungs and her body reacted spectacularly, a million miles away from what her head was trying to impose on it. She felt a tremor start in her legs.

She had completely forgotten about Dominic until she heard him behind her. 'Janey, love, are you all right? Do you know this man?'

She came out of her reverie.

'Yes.'

She let Xavier pass her to come into the small hall, feeling a hysterical giggle bubbling up from somewhere deep in her belly.

'Dominic, this is Xavier Salgado-Lézille. Xavier, this is Dominic Miller—an old friend of mine.'

The men looked at each other with deep suspicion. Jane knew she had to put Dominic out of his misery. She threw a quelling look at Xavier and showed him into the sitting room, shutting the door behind him.

Leading Dominic away from the door, she said, 'Xavier is my baby's father…and it wouldn't be fair to take you up on your offer because…' her voice gentled '…I'm not in love with you.'

'Are you in love with him?'

She nodded her head mutely.

'Is he in love with you?'

She shook her head. 'But he will take care of me and the baby if I so wish. I know that. You don't have to worry about me.'

She pressed a kiss to his cheek, making him colour again.

'Are you sure you're OK…? I can stay if you want.'

Jane shook her head, ignoring her rapid pulse. Dominic was no match for Xavier.

She let him out, the difference in the two men comical as they passed in the hallway. At the sitting room door took a deep breath before going in.

Xavier was pacing the small room, dwarfing it with his size and presence.

'Who was that?'

She bristled at the proprietorial tone in his voice, hating the effect he was having on her.

'He's my best friend's brother.'

'What did he want?'

'It's none of your business what he wanted.' She sat down to disguise the trembling in her legs, then contradicted herself, saying disbelievingly, 'As a matter of fact, he asked me to marry him.'

'Did you say yes… *Janey, love*?' Xavier's voice was sharp.

She looked up. His face was shuttered, his eyes giving nothing away. Her heart twisted at the mocking way he repeated Dominic's friendly endearment.

'What's it to you? I can marry whoever I want.'

He hauled her up against his chest so quickly that she didn't have time to protest before his mouth descended and his lips found hers. After a second of shock she was like someone dying of thirst who had found water in the desert. With a small whimper she wrapped her arms around his neck, and their tongues collided in a heated feverish dance.

Time stood still.

She was home.

Then he thrust her away from him.

'*That's* why it's my business. You're carrying my baby—and don't tell me you react like that with everyone.'

Shocked blue eyes clashed with blistering green.

'That's why, if you marry anyone, it'll be me. No one

else. Our baby deserves to be brought up within a marriage. He is going to be my heir, and as such will be afforded the necessary ceremony for his inheritance.'

The shock of what he was suggesting rendered her speechless for a moment.

'I will not marry you just for the sake of an heir. Don't be so ridiculous... It would be a sham...and anyway it could be a girl,' she pointed out somewhat pedantically.

He threw off his overcoat and jacket, loosening his tie. He was like a panther in a confined space. Hands on hips.

'Boy or girl... You would deny our child—possibly the only child I may ever have—its inheritance?'

Jane gasped. 'Are you threatening me? That if I don't marry you then you will effectively deny its existence?'

'It won't be up to me... Before my father died he added a codicil to his will stating that should I have any children outside marriage they wouldn't be entitled to anything. It was his way of ensuring the line would continue in our family's name, ensuring that the island stays in the family.' He shrugged. 'He was very conservative, and there's no way around it.'

She had a sudden memory of the numerous pictures of Xavier with countless women in the press, and words tumbled out, barely coherent to her muddled brain.

'You've had to check that out already? Maybe you have other children dotted around the world—Milan, Paris—?'

He took her by the shoulders. 'No, I don't. I don't make a habit of jumping in and out of bed with countless partners, and I always make sure I'm protected.... Just with you...with you something happened.'

His hands were biting into her shoulders. Something had happened, all right, and she could see how much he hated to admit it. It was in every strained line in his face. He had been taken over by the lust of the moment, whereas she had been taken over by much, much more. She could remember all too well what had happened. She had let good sense out and madness in. She tried to avoid his probing gaze.

'OK...maybe you don't, but what you're suggesting is positively medieval. Surely in this day and age—'

'Did you really think I'd just walk away? I'm offering you everything on a plate...security, respectability, a name for our child.'

Everything but yourself... This heir is everything to him... as important as she had suspected.

She sought for rational words in a brain that was fast becoming fuzzier and fuzzier. 'He or she could still take your name, if it's that important. I can't...please don't make me...'

'There's no need to go green. It doesn't have to be a completely unpleasant experience. We're still attracted to each other—you can't deny feeling it too, the minute you walked into my office today.'

He didn't have to remind her of that mortifying fact. She brought huge wary eyes up to his. 'Yes, but that's all, isn't it?'

His face was expressionless. He shrugged negligently. 'It's more than a lot of people start out with. Jane, I'm thirty-six. It's time I got married and produced an heir.'

She felt a hysterical laugh bubble up again. 'It's almost as if I've fallen in with some cosmic plan to save your family legacy.'

The lines in his face were harsh, and suddenly she didn't feel like laughing. This was all too real.

'Don't mock me, Jane. There aren't many women who would turn down an offer like this.'

Even though his words reeked with arrogance, she didn't doubt for a second that what he said was true. She just happened to hold the ace. His seed inside her belly. Lucky her. She had pipped all the contenders to the post. She tried another tack.

'Yes, but most people start out with love, however misguided...at least it's there to start.'

'And where does it leave them in the end? At least we would be going into this with eyes open—without the illusion of love to cloud things. I believe we have something we can work on, Jane. I wouldn't suggest it otherwise.'

She shifted out from under his hands and sank back down onto the couch, feeling hunted.

Something we can work on...

She knew all too well what he meant. It saturated the air around them.

He hunched down before her, not letting her evade his compelling gaze. 'Jane, the future of Lézille is at stake if I don't provide an heir. This could be my only child.'

She looked at him, helpless.

The doorbell rang again. Xavier went to answer it. She didn't even notice. But she did when she heard the voices. Her mother and Arthur. She closed her eyes. It couldn't get any worse.

Her mother came into the room with one brow arched so high that it almost met her hairline.

'Hello, Mum.' Jane hugged her, feeling the onset of tears in her maternal presence.

She quickly made the introductions, without saying precisely who Xavier was, but she could see that her mother had deduced exactly what his role was.

Unbelievably, Xavier offered to go into the kitchen to make some tea, leaving them alone for a few minutes and making her feel even more confused. How could he come in here and take over so effortlessly? Her mother and Arthur were certainly looking after him with barely disguised awe.

'So that's...?' Arthur nodded in the direction of Xavier's retreating back.

Jane nodded miserably.

'Well, darling, you don't look very happy about it,' her mother whispered.

I'm not!

Her mother and Arthur looked at each other before linking hands. The lump grew in her throat again.

'Dear…we've had a long think, and we came to tell you that if you're still determined to go it alone…we're going to stay here in England.'

Jane started to protest and her mother shushed her, holding up a hand. 'Now, I know what you're going to say, but it's decided… There is no way we can leave you here on your own to bring up that child, and that's final.'

Despite the encouraging smiles on their faces, she could see how hard it had been for them to make this decision. And there was no way she could let them. Her Mum's happiness involved Arthur too. And right now they came first. She could mess up her own life, but not the life of this woman in front of her, who had sacrificed so much already.

She heard Xavier's step approach the sitting room and knew what she had to do. She went with her gut. In that split second she knew she was about to make a choice that was going to change her life. She hoped and prayed that it was the right one. She didn't have time to consider the ramifications.

He came in to the room with a laden tray. Jane waited until he had put it down and the tea was passed out before speaking, and tried to keep a steady voice.

'Mum, Arthur…I really appreciate what you want to do for me, but you see there's no need.'

She glanced at Xavier's ever unreadable face. She wasn't going to get any help there. She took a deep breath.

'You don't have to stay here because…you see…I'm not going to be here.'

Her mother and Arthur looked at each other blankly, then at Xavier and then at her.

'What are you talking about, dear?'

Jane mentally crossed her fingers and took poetic licence with her recent conversation with Xavier. 'Xavier has asked me to marry him…and I am going to say…yes.'

She could hear a splutter of tea come from his corner of the room. Then she was enveloped in hugs and tears and congratulations. Xavier joined in and answered questions vaguely. She was very aware of his sharp, assessing eyes on her all the time.

She knew she had done the right thing, however, when she saw the badly disguised relief on their faces at the prospect that their dream would be fulfilled after all.

Finally, after what seemed an age, they were gone. She went back into the sitting room to find Xavier standing at the window. He turned around and fixed her with hard eyes.

'I gather that little charade was for the benefit of persuading your mother that she and her husband could emigrate after all?'

'Well, it's not going to be a charade unless you won't marry me.'

He approached her softly, coming dangerously close. 'If you were trying to call my bluff then it didn't work. We *will* be getting married. I suppose I should have thanked your mother for helping you to come to your decision…' He gave a short harsh laugh. 'You couldn't have made it clearer that it's the last thing you'd be doing otherwise.'

'You're right. I hate you for this.' Her chest felt tight and restricted, her hands clammy.

A savage intensity flashed over his face so briefly that she might have imagined it before it was gone, and he drawled, 'That hate will just fuel our passion…because it is still there.'

She vowed there and then that there would be no passion. If he so much as touched her, she wasn't sure that she could contain her feelings—and if he guessed for a second…her life would be hell.

He left with a promise to return and discuss things in the morning, and after the door shut behind him Jane sagged against it, the stuffing knocked out of her.

Despite everything that had just transpired, somewhere

within herself she felt curiously at peace. Was she so straight that once she had agreed to doing 'the right thing' she felt good? It couldn't be. What was more likely, she feared, was that she was such a masochist that even though being married to Xavier spelt certain heartbreak, it also meant she got to be with him…and seeing him again had proved how completely he held her heart in his hands.

The baby. How could she deny this little person access to his or her father? To their birth heritage? Especially one so rich—and not just in monetary terms. She knew instinctively that Xavier would be a good father.

Her mind went a more incendiary route. Would he be faithful if she refused to sleep with him? A man as virile and highly sexed as Xavier would not stand for a celibate marriage. How could she hope to live side by side with him and resist him? All she knew was that she had to, for now. Her emotions were too raw…too close to the surface. Maybe in time, when they were more under control, she could… remain detached. As if there ever could be such a time.

She went to bed with a heavy heart and slept fitfully.

The next morning when she opened the door to admit Xavier he took in her pinched face and the dark smudges under her eyes. The pang that struck him when he realised that he was the one who was making her look this unhappy gripped him unawares. He quashed it ruthlessly.

Jane eyed him warily with crossed arms as he effortlessly commanded her small flat again. He was dressed in a suit that hugged his frame, making him seem even more powerful, dynamic. He looked exotic and foreign, his tan standing out against the grimly grey backdrop outside. Stupendously gorgeous.

'I've arranged for us to be married here in London in just over two weeks time at a register office. It's the earliest I could arrange... Also it should be easier for your mother and Arthur to attend before they leave for South Africa. If there's anyone else you want to witness it...'

His efficiency and ability to make the powers that be fall into his plans stunned her—and his unexpected sensitivity to accommodate her mother.

'Well, yes...' She thought of Lisa. 'There's one or two people, maybe...'

'*Bien*. I have to go to New York today, and will be gone until the day of the wedding, so I trust that will give you time to pack up here, tie up any loose ends and inform your work. Molly can arrange to have this place let or sold, whichever you prefer.'

She spoke quickly. 'Let...that is, I don't want to sell it.'

Somehow the thought of severing all ties was too much just now.

He shrugged as if he didn't care.

'Fine. As you wish. I'll let her know she can go ahead with arrangements and find a suitable agent?'

Jane nodded dumbly.

'After the wedding we will stop over in Paris for a short honeymoon. We can replenish your wardrobe there.' He eyed her casual attire critically. 'You'll have a certain role to fulfil as my wife, and will need to be dressed suitably.'

His bossy tone was too much.

'I think I know how to dress myself, thank you very much... You don't have to spend your money on me.'

'Very commendable, darling, but somehow I don't think you could afford even the price tags on the kind of clothes I'm talking about,' he drawled, with infuriating arrogance.

'Fine...' She threw her hands up. 'If you want to spend thousands on making me into something I will never be except on paper, then go ahead and be my guest.'

He came and stood right in front of her. She could feel his breath warm on her face. Her heart lurched as he drifted a finger down one cheek and underneath to her neck, where her pulse was beating crazily against her skin.

'Oh, but you will, Jane…you will. Trust me on that.'

CHAPTER NINE

Two weeks later Jane was trying to contain herself as she felt an increasing sense of panic threaten to overwhelm her. Lisa and her mother fussed around her as she got ready to go to the register office, their chatter skimming over her head:

'...and poor Dominic is heartbroken, but he happened to mention that Xavier is gorgeous...'

'Oh, he is, dear—wait till you see him...'

'And he really owns a whole island?'

'That's nothing...his hotel chain...'

'Still waters, eh, Mrs V? Who would have thought our little Janey had it in her? And to think of all those holidays spent with him under my nose—the time I wasted on those waiters...'

Jane cut in with wry exasperation. 'You know, I *am* here, guys.'

'Yes, dear, don't mind us...now, let's have a look at you.'

She was wearing a fitted cream silk jacket and a matching skirt that was cut on the bias and fell in soft swinging folds to her knees. The material clung to her curves, and the buttons on the jacket closed under her bust, with a lace camisole just visible in a slightly darker shade of off-white. An effective camouflage for her thickening middle.

Her mother hadn't grilled her too much since her revelations and announcement. She assumed she and Xavier had

had some sort of lovers' tiff, and was blithely unaware of the circumstances—which Jane was quite happy with.

She contemplated the rest of the outfit—sheer tights, and high heels covered in the same material as the suit. It wasn't bad for the last minute. Lisa had secured her hair with a flower, and stood back to regard her subject, resplendent herself in a vibrant hot pink dress that clashed magnificently with her red hair.

'Janey, you look like a model… Honestly, what I wouldn't give for your height and figure… When I get pregnant I'm going to be the proverbial whale from day one.'

Right now Jane would have given anything to switch places with Lisa. But of course she couldn't. She had to do this, for the baby and to ensure her mother and Arthur's future. And if she was honest she had to acknowledge the dark part of her that *wanted* to go through with this—wanted to tie herself to Xavier, whatever the cost.

When she saw him standing at the table in front of the registrar she faltered for a moment, her nerve failing her, but in that instant he turned and saw her. They hadn't seen each other since that morning in her flat. It all fell away. Some intensity in his eyes held her. Didn't allow her to break contact. She looked neither left nor right, just went towards him as if he was some kind of homing beacon in a fog. Then she was next to him. It was only the voice of the registrar that brought her back into room and their surroundings.

The words were meaningless. She hoped she made the appropriate response at the right time because she felt disembodied from everything. Before she knew it Xavier was taking a ring from his pocket and placing it on her finger, his hands cool and steady. Then, remarkably, Lisa was handing her a ring—where had that come from?

Jane put it on his finger, it slid on effortlessly. He didn't let go of her hand until the end of the ceremony.

Once it was over they went outside. Xavier told her that

he had arranged for a celebratory breakfast to be held at his London hotel. He led her to a waiting chauffeur-driven Bentley. She could see that there were more people than she had initially noticed, and that there were cars lined up for everyone. He had organised all this?

In the back of the car they were alone once he indicated to the driver to raise the partition. He brought a couple of glasses from a hidden compartment and poured them both some sparkling water. She couldn't help but be aware of his huge frame encased in the dark grey morning suit. The material stretched over hard thighs only inches from hers.

'A poor replacement for champagne, but necessary.'

Jane didn't want him to guess how her insides were churning, the confused anger and frustration she felt at his matter-of-fact tone.

'Let's drink to us.'

'A bit of a lie, don't you, think? There's no one around to fool.'

'Let's drink to a truce, then, because we're sure as hell not going to last one week if you stay in that filthy mood. You've looked like you were going to your own funeral since you arrived.'

Hot tears threatened. She clinked his glass and took a sip, feeling like a fraud.

'I'm sorry…it's just a little overwhelming… Within weeks of seeing you again I'm married and about to emigrate…'

He surprised her by taking her hand in his and lifting it to his mouth. The heat of his lips pressed to her skin made her insides melt. Along with the look in his eyes.

'Don't think about it now…let's just get through the next few days. It's not exactly been easy for me either, you know.'

For a moment they shared an intense communication. There was something in his face…but then it was gone. A bland expression replaced whatever it was, and Jane couldn't help but feel he was talking about being forced into a marriage he didn't want. She reminded herself how single-minded he was. He hadn't even made an attempt for them to talk about things, get to know one another again. He'd taken off as soon as he knew she'd comply with his demands, spent the last two weeks in New York, and come back only at the last minute. Arrogantly sure of her response.

The car drew to a smooth halt outside the hotel, and they were ushered out and into the melee.

Jane was introduced to so many people that they were soon blurring into one, and her cheeks ached from smiling. Her feet ached too, and for the first time since becoming pregnant she felt exhausted. She was ever conscious of Xavier, and where he was. Whenever she caught his eye he held it for long moments, until she began to get flustered and looked away.

She had just seen off her mother, Arthur and Lisa, whose own parents had come too. Jane had been delighted to see Lisa's dad, looking so well after his scare. Her friend had promised to visit soon, and her mother was planning on coming when the baby was born.

Standing alone in the doorway of the function room, she felt awkward with all these unknown people. Some of them were friends of Xavier's and seemed perfectly nice; others were business acquaintances.

Suddenly he materialised at her side, slipping an arm around her waist, and for once she sank gratefully into him, glad of the support.

'Let's get out of here,' he murmured into her ear.

'Yes, please.' She couldn't disguise the relief in her voice.

He brought her up to the penthouse suite. The staff had left out a bottle of champagne and there were rose petals all over the bed.

What a waste…

She turned to face Xavier as he closed and locked the door. He came towards her, pulling off his bow tie and opening his shirt. She could see his eyes darkening and saw the intention in them. It reached out and caressed her across the room, and she could feel every part of herself respond. It was too much. Her feelings were too raw. She backed away.

'Xavier…please. I'm tired…I want to go to sleep.'

He kept coming. 'So do I. With you.'

'No!' She hadn't meant for her voice to come out so strident. 'Just…I need a little space, and I am exhausted.'

She had been exhausted earlier, but now an excess of energy was causing her body to hum, making a lie of her words. Since seeing him again an ache had settled into every cell, an ache that she knew only he could assuage. He stopped in his tracks and she wanted to throw caution to the wind, throw herself at him with an animalistic instinct…rip off his clothes, have him take her right where they were. The strength of her reaction shook her.

'I don't know what you're playing at, but I'll give you the benefit of the doubt for now. I'll go back downstairs for a while. You take the bed…I'll sleep on the couch.'

'Xavier, there's no need—'

'Save it, Jane. If you think we can share that bed tonight without anything happening then you're lying to yourself.'

The door closed ominously quietly behind him.

Jane began to get ready for bed, feeling even more miserable. As if she had somehow cut off her nose to spite her face. Her body still hadn't cooled down since that electrifying look.

She sped through her toilet in record time, and was soon under the sheets, breathing harshly and feeling very silly. After waiting as long as she could, she finally gave in to her exhaustion and slept, not hearing her bedroom door open or Xavier come in and spend long moments looking at her.

The next day on Xavier's private jet, as they flew to Paris, she tried to control her conflicting emotions. She studied him covertly from under her lashes, and twisted the slim white-gold band on her finger as he looked through some paperwork in the seat across the aisle from her. He looked totally at ease, with not a care in the world. Unlike her. She looked out of her window and tried to force herself to relax.

What seemed like only moments later she felt someone shaking her gently. It was Xavier. His face was very close to hers. She could see the darker flecks of green in his eyes. It brought back a vivid image of his pupils dilating as his head descended to hers before he took her mouth with his. She hunched back in the seat to escape the potent memory.

He frowned at her movement. 'What…what is it?' she asked, her voice strained.

'We're here…in Paris.'

She looked out of the window. Sure enough they were on the Tarmac; she could see a waiting limo just at the bottom of the steps. None of the usual Customs or red tape for Xavier and his wife.

Once in the limo, it wasn't long before they were in the thick of traffic in the city. Jane looked out with undisguised awe.

'Have you never been here before?' Xavier asked incredulously.

She shook her head. 'Never had time…or the money. When I left school I worked straight away through college. I wanted to start paying Mum back for all the years that she'd worked her fingers to the bone.'

'If I didn't already know you I'd say that was a line…'

Jane looked at him, shaking her head. 'So cynical…how can you bear it?'

'Not everyone sees the world through rose-tinted glasses.'

'Well, mine are rapidly turning more opaque.'

She could feel his sharp look of enquiry, but didn't elaborate.

She picked out the Eiffel Tower, Notre Dame…and before long she could see that they were going over an ornate bridge on to what looked like an island in the middle of the river.

'Wow…' she breathed.

'This is the Île St-Louis—one of a few islands on the Seine…it's mainly residential.'

I'll say, Jane thought to herself. Chic, immaculately made-up women walked their beautifully coiffed dogs. And she had thought that image of Paris was such a cliché!

They drew to a smooth halt outside one of the buildings and were effusively greeted by the doorman. Jane was fast becoming accustomed again to the bowing and scraping people did in Xavier's vicinity. In the lift she wasn't surprised to see that they went all the way to the top floor. Nothing but the best.

The doors opened straight into a hall with one door, which Xavier opened.

'This is where I come and stay when in Paris on business or for stopovers on long haul journeys—have a look around.'

Jane tore her eyes away from his and did as he asked. It was the quintessential bachelor pad. The age of the building meant that the shell and windows were still of a certain period, but the whole of the inside had been remodelled. The colours were dark, and it was full of sharp corners, with abstract art on the walls, state-of-the-art sound and TV systems. The kitchen was worse, all gleaming steel and not a hint of homeliness in sight. She hated it.

He stood back, arms folded, and watched her face with amusement. She couldn't hide a thing. He felt a sharp, uncustomary burst of pleasure, remembering her refreshing honesty, and became aware of just how much he had missed it…

'You hate it, don't you?'

'I'm sorry…' She blushed. 'It's just so cold and characterless.'

And he became aware of how he'd missed her blushes.

'I suppose I'd be offended if I'd actually had a hand in the decoration, but thankfully for my ego I didn't. I allowed a friend who was trying to build up his interior design portfolio the run of the place. I'm here so infrequently that it doesn't really bother me.'

He thought of the women that he had brought here. He couldn't remember one who hadn't oohed and ahed delightedly over every room. Either they had all loved it or, more realistically, said what they thought he wanted to hear. Now he could see it through Jane's eyes he hated it too, and vowed to rip it all out and do it up again.

Her heart hammered when he suddenly took her hand. He led her to a bedroom, where he faced her again.

'What…what are you doing?' she asked desperately, hating the effect just holding his hand was having on her, but determined not to pull away and reveal the extent of her discomfiture.

He indicated with his head round the room, starkly decorated in creams and browns. 'This is your room.'

The relief on her face was comic. 'Thank…thank you.'

He rested heavy hands on her shoulders. 'Your hands-off signals are loud and clear. Rest assured, Jane, I've never forced myself on a woman and I'm not about to now…but you know you're fighting a losing battle, don't you? This scared virginal act is wasted on me. We both know you're no virgin.'

He brought his face down to hers, his mouth close to her ear, and she closed her eyes weakly. His breath tickled the sensitive part of her neck just below her ear. The fine hairs standing up.

'But if you think for a second that you can hold out for ever…then you're very, very mistaken. It's only going to be a matter of time. It's there, vibrating between us like an electric current, and it's not going to go away. Do you know what happens when you suppress something? It just gets stronger and stronger.'

He straightened up, his eyes taking in her flushed face, the bead of sweat on her brow, the pulse hammering against the base of her neck, and he had to use every ounce of his will-power not to pull her into him, mould her body to his and make her acquiesce—which he knew he could do.

He would wait until she was shaking with longing, weak with desire. Until she could barely look at him because of it. He wanted her. Badly. But that was all it was. Sheer, unadulterated lust. Nothing else. This was why he'd been unable to get her out of his head the past few months.

'Settle in, and I'll get lunch ready.'

He walked out of the room. Jane pressed her hands up against flaming cheeks. That was her reaction after mere words! What would she do if he kissed her? Or if she lost control and grabbed him? Which seemed more likely right at that moment. She'd go up like tumbleweed to a lit match on a dry day.

All the more reason to be strong.

And what then…?

One day at a time. That was the only way she was going to handle this.

CHAPTER TEN

THE next morning Xavier insisted on a day of sightseeing.

In the early evening they emerged from the Louvre. Jane was bone weary, even though the ever-present limo had whisked them from place to place.

Bone weary because at every opportunity during the day he had touched her—usually just the slightest glance of physical contact, a brush of a hand here, a light touch on her waist or shoulder…pressing close against her in the crowds. But it had been enough to set her nerve-ends jangling, almost as though he knew exactly what he was doing. His face each time she'd sneaked a look had shown pure innocence.

By the time he took her hand outside the great museum she was worn down from trying to escape him, and just left it in his without a word. That contact, chaste as it was, was torture in itself.

'I let Pascal go home… There's a restaurant near here I thought might be nice for dinner. We can get a cab later.'

'I'm not dressed properly…' She indicated her jeans and sneakers.

'Don't worry, it's a low-key place.'

She shrugged and allowed him to lead her through the streets. They came to a charming little bistro, tucked into a small side street, with only a few tables that were already full.

Xavier was greeted like a long-lost son by the proprietor,

and when he introduced Jane as his wife there were shouts and a woman came running out. Jane was enveloped in hugs and warm kisses, and couldn't help but be charmed. The older woman at one point looked at Jane's ring finger and unleashed a stream of French at Xavier that Jane couldn't follow. He looked shamefaced after it.

Once they were seated at a free table that had appeared as if by magic, Jane had to ask, 'What on earth did she say to you?'

'Madame Feron pointed out that you don't have an engagement ring.'

Jane lifted her hand stupidly. 'Oh…I hadn't even thought about it myself.' She looked back to him. 'I don't need one, you know…it'd be silly just for the sake of it. Plenty of people nowadays just wear a wedding band.'

'Nevertheless, she's right. We will do this properly. I'll buy you one tomorrow.'

His tone brooked no argument. His businesslike attitude reinforced her will to resist him at all costs. This was nothing more than a mutual agreement, each having their own reasons: him to secure his heir and its future, her for the baby's sake and to secure her mother's future in South Africa.

But maybe down the road when the baby was born they could negotiate a separation? Surely by then any inheritance would be safe? Jane knew in her heart of hearts that sooner or later her will would break, or Xavier would succumb to another woman, and either scenario would be untenable for long. She knew that now, as she looked at him across the table.

Her appetite still wasn't back to normal, but she forced the food down, not wanting to insult the couple who couldn't stop beaming at them.

That night when they got back to the apartment Jane fled into her room as soon as she could. She rested against the door, breathing heavily with eyes closed. She heard Xavier's step pausing outside her door and her mouth went dry, her pulse tripping.

'Goodnight…' he called softly through the door.

But he may as well have said *coward*. It was what he meant.

She got under the covers a short while later and pulled them over her head, as if that would block out the images, the vivid memories that played like a home movie every night in her dreams. Her body felt as though it had a fever. What was wrong with her? She was pregnant…how could she be feeling so…so…*sexually aware* of herself and him?

She slept fitfully. Again.

The following morning Xavier informed her that they would spend the day shopping and return to the island that evening. When he saw the less than enthusiastic expression on her face he frowned.

'What is it? Are you feeling ill?'

'No…it's nothing…just that I've always hated shopping. The crowds…trying things on. It bores me to tears. But as you say, I have to keep up appearances now.'

He shook his head, once again struck dumb. Reminded of how different she was from the women he was used to.

An hour or so later, when they approached the door of a designer shop, Jane caught his hand and dragged him back. The memory of years of scrimping and saving rushed back in lurid humiliating detail, her mother's face lined with worry and strain as she struggled to let down another hem, trying to get another year out of a school skirt.

'We can't go in there…those clothes cost a fortune. Look, why don't you just let me go off for a few hours? I'll find some high street stores and kit myself out. Honestly, you can trust me…'

'Woman!' he exploded, stunning her into silence. 'I'm normally dragged on these expeditions, reduced to nothing more than a walking credit card, but you—' He shook his head. 'You have to have morals. Jane, without insulting your intelligence too much, will you please trust me when I say that if I let you go off and *kit yourself out*, as you put it, within weeks we will be at some function where it will be horrendously obvious to everyone that I can't afford to dress my own wife. This isn't just for you. As much as I agree with your sensibilities, unfortunately society hasn't caught up with us, and I have a certain standard to maintain.'

Her mouth opened and closed ineffectually, a red-hot poker of pain striking her at his reference to what must have been many other trips like this…with other women he had indulged. She walked into the shop without another word, hoping to distract him from her hurt.

By that afternoon she'd lost count of the shops… Dresses, casual clothes, shoes, underwear—which thankfully he had absented himself for—and last but not least maternity wear. She had worked very hard at putting images of other women out of her head, and berated herself for not expecting as much in the first place.

Xavier had arranged for everything to be sent straight to the plane and loaded up. Once they were on it themselves, later that day, Jane felt a pang of guilt mixed with fear. Xavier saw the look on her face.

'What is it?'

She shook her head rapidly. 'Nothing…nothing at all.'

Everything!

She averted her head and looked out of the window. When she thought about the afternoon she had to admit that she had enjoyed it on some level. Who wouldn't have? Assistants fawning all over her. Well, over Xavier's credit card, to be accurate. And what on the surface must have looked like a doting husband indulging his new bride. The covetous looks of the other women hadn't gone unnoticed. At one point she had even felt the old warmth creep up, when one of the women had been particularly sycophantic. Jane had looked to Xavier and caught his identical look, and a bubble of delighted communication had almost transformed her face, made her forget why she was there. But that would be far too dangerous. What they had shared in the summer was not who he really was. She had to remember that.

Once the small plane was cruising, and the seat belt signs were off, she saw Xavier turn towards her from the corner of her eye.

'Jane, I have something for you.'

She turned to look.

'More? What could you possibly—?'

She went silent when she saw him reach into the inside pocket of his jacket and pull out a small box, which he offered her across the aisle. She looked at him and her hands shook slightly as took it. When she opened it she gasped. Nestled in a bed of cream velvet was the most stunning sapphire ring in an antique square setting of tiny diamonds and white-gold. It was beautiful. How could he have picked exactly what she would have gone for herself?

'How did you know…?'

'I remembered something you told me once about sapphires being your favourite stone…'

She couldn't help but be touched that he had remembered.

'We can change it if you don't like it,' he said stiffly.

She looked up quickly. 'I lo—' She stopped herself and amended her words. 'It's beautiful.'

She put it on her finger with a tremor in her hand. A perfect fit.

He went back to his papers; she went back to looking out of the window, with the sting of tears in her eyes at the sterility of the exchange.

They landed at the private air strip on Lézille in the early evening.

Xavier's four-wheel drive was parked nearby, and he expertly negotiated his way out of the tiny airstrip and towards the castle, silhouetted on the horizon against a darkening sky.

This time it wasn't empty. A retinue of people were lined up to welcome them home. Most of the names and faces were a blur as Jane struggled to hang onto them. A gardener, cook, maid…and at the head of the queue Xavier introduced her with obvious affection to Jean-Paul and Yvette who, he told her, had run the castle since he was a baby. They had the same dark distinctively Spanish features of the rest of the islanders.

Before she knew what was happening, Xavier had lifted her up to carry her over the threshold. When he put her down again she stood back, trembling and breathing hard…disconcerted. Another tear threatened….for about the third time that day. She told herself it must be her hormones, emotions too close to the surface. She couldn't read his face, searching desperately for some indication that his motivation wasn't ironic. Or an act purely for the staff, who were looking on delightedly. She had to admit that was more likely. But his face was shuttered, expressionless. She controlled her wayward reactions.

Yvette shyly led Jane upstairs to the master bedroom. It all looked familiar, and exactly how she remembered it. Little had she known that she'd ever be back…married and pregnant. She sank onto the side of the bed and looked around, feeling a little removed from everything. Her life had changed so completely within just a few months, a total one-hundred-and-eighty-degree turn. Goosebumps prickled across her skin and she wrapped her arms around herself, feeling a sudden chill.

She went to look out of the window. The scenery was as vividly breathtaking as she remembered, just slightly less lush than it had been in the summer.

A movement out of the corner of her eye made her look round. Xavier had appeared in the door, holding one of her bags.

With sudden panic and clarity she realised something. 'Xavier…this is your room.'

'Yes. And now it's your room too.'

He walked in, closing the door behind him, coming uncomfortably close. Jane wrapped her arms tighter around herself, forcing herself to remain calm. But it was difficult. The bed in the corner of her eye loomed large and threatening; the memories were rushing back.

'We are not sleeping together.'

'Yes, we are.' He enunciated each word with chilling softness.

'No.'

He ran an angry hand through his hair and Jane could feel the energy crackle around them. 'Jane, we are going to share this room if I have to lock us both in here every night. If the staff see us sleeping separately, word of a fractured marriage will spread before morning. And I will not have that. We may as well not have bothered getting married.'

Jane threw her hands in the air and moved away jerkily, pacing back and forth. 'Don't be ridiculous. If I sleep in the other room I can make sure the sheets are pristine every morning…I'll—'

'Now you're being ridiculous. Tell me, Jane…why the great resistance? Don't you remember how it was between us?'

Didn't she remember?

Her stomach dropped with sudden panic under his narrowed gaze. Resisting him…and this overwhelming desire…was the only way she knew how to protect herself. He *couldn't* ever know…and if he started to look at her motives…

She wouldn't even contemplate that scenario. She placed a protective hand on her belly. It might as well have been over her heart. She mustered up a look that would have frozen boiling water, her blue eyes chips of ice,

'This baby is the only thing I care about. I'm pregnant, Xavier, I don't feel those…*urges*.'

She hated using the baby like this, but she needed all the armour she could get. Anything that would keep him at a distance. She knew that he would not step over the line…

unless she gave the word. Which she was determined not to—until she knew she could stay detached, if such a time existed.

A savage intensity flashed over his face. The hell she didn't feel those *urges*. Every part of her quivered lightly before him; she was taut as a bow, just waiting for his touch. His eyes dropped to the hand over her belly, before they took in the rise and fall of her chest. He wanted to walk over and shake her, and call her a liar to her face. He caught her darting a glance to the bed, the slight flush under her skin. He moved closer.

She backed away.

He gestured to the bed, taking in her reluctance to follow his gaze with something akin to triumph. 'It's a king-size bed. Plenty of room for two people on opposite sides to never come close to touching.'

'I don't trust you. No way.' She eyed him warily from under her lashes, arms back around her body.

'Oh, Jane, be honest…it's not me you don't trust, it's yourself.'

Of all the conceited…!

Jane's blood boiled; her arms dropped. 'Fine. If you can keep your hands to yourself, then I certainly won't have a problem keeping my hands off *you*.'

'Good.' He smiled smugly. 'I'm going to catch up on some calls. Yvette will bring the rest of your things up shortly, so you can get settled in.'

When he left the room Jane could have kicked herself for allowing him to goad her. But she couldn't back down. Somehow she knew it would be more dangerous if he suspected for a second what she suspected herself. That he was absolutely right about her not trusting herself to share his bed. He was playing a game with her, she knew. She would not be the one to crack.

But in a deep, dark corner she was very much afraid that she would indeed be the one to crack…

CHAPTER ELEVEN

'I PRESUME you won't mind me leaving you to make some calls, as you've barely said two words over dinner…?'

Jane looked up sharply. In contrast to her tense form, spine as straight as a dancer's, he lounged at the opposite side of the table, long legs stretched out, a brow quirked mockingly.

'Not at all…' she replied sweetly.

The heavy potent atmosphere was giving her a headache. She was more than uncomfortably aware of him. His scent, his large body mere inches away across the table. During dinner she'd been transfixed by his hands, until she'd realised she was staring. Still in a state of shock to be back here…with him…again.

In a way, she reflected when he'd taken his leave and her pulse had finally returned to normal, it would be easier to have people around. It would have been too much to have the slumberous heat outside and the entire place to themselves. Things were more formal with the staff here. There was none of the seductive easy intimacy of the summer…making dinner in the kitchen, eating outside. The outer changes just reflected their own inner reality. Everything was different.

She went up to the bedroom and changed into the most un-revealing nightwear she had—a pair of silk pyjamas—buttoning them up as far as possible, and automatically went to the side of the bed that she'd used before, aghast at how natural it felt.

Scooting down under the covers, she felt her body rigid with tension, and she lay like that for at least an hour, until she heard his footfall and the door open. She stopped breathing, her eyes shut tight as he came into the room.

Forcing herself to take long shallow breaths, it was torture as she heard his movements and tried not to imagine what he was doing. The whisper of a shirt sliding off, a belt buckle opened, a button being popped. When she heard his trousers hit the floor, and the barely discernible sound of his underwear being tugged down, a corresponding heat flooded her lower belly. She had to bite her lip to keep back a moan.

She heard his footsteps pad to the bathroom and water running, being turned off, and then the footsteps come back to the bed. She felt the dip as he pulled the covers back and got in. She was curled in a ball, as far away from him as she could get, the covers tucked around her like a wall.

She only fell asleep once he'd stopped moving and she heard his deep breaths even out.

When Jane woke the next morning she was in the same position she'd fallen asleep in, and she could feel how the tension had cramped her muscles. With a wary look over her shoulder, she breathed out when she saw that Xavier was already up, the sheet pulled neatly back. She took advantage of the solitude and got up, taking a quick shower and dressing before going downstairs, meeting Yvette on the way.

'Oh, *madame*! You should have stayed in bed. You must be tired…I was going to bring you breakfast.'

Jane smiled warmly at her. 'There's no need. I'm sure you have enough to be doing…I'll come and get something in the kitchen myself.'

She looked up over Yvette's head and saw Xavier at the bottom of the stairs, watching her intently. She could see a muscle work in his jaw from where she was. Had he slept well last night? She searched his face for signs, but he looked remarkably well. Vibrant. She proceeded down the stairs, fighting to look cool.

'Morning.'

'Morning.'

'Did you—?'

'I hope you—'

They both spoke at the same time, and Jane took the lead, saying airily, 'Oh, like a log. I didn't even hear you come in. Was it late?'

He took her arm and led her across the hall before leaning down close and breathing into her ear, 'Liar.'

Before she could react, and quell the butterflies he'd set off in her stomach, he straightened and said in a normal voice, 'We have visitors to see you, darling…' He looked back to Yvette. 'The Vercors are here. Bring some tea and a selection of things please…' He dropped his voice again as he walked her to the door of the sitting room. 'I remember what a large appetite you have, even if you don't want to.'

Her mouth was open and her face pink when he manoeuvred her into the bright room. He smiled benignly down into her face.

'Darling, do you remember Sophie Vercors? And this is her husband Paul.'

Jane forced herself to tear her eyes away from his mesmerising pull and looked at the couple. She immediately recalled the glamorous woman from that day when they'd bumped into her on the road, on the way down to the beach. The sudden memory of it had her cheeks flame red.

She stood to greet Jane warmly. Xavier's hand on her back propelled her forward.

'Jane! It's good to see you again…I had a funny feeling I might.'

Sophie's eyes twinkled with mischief, and Jane found herself responding to her warmth gratefully.

'And this is my darling husband, Paul.'

She pulled the man forward. He was quite a bit older than Sophie, balding and with a definite paunch, but he had the kindest eyes and a look of mischief to match his wife's. It was clear, despite their mismatched appearances, that they loved each other deeply.

'Shame on you, Xavier, for getting married in London… and the baby! What great news…'

Xavier slanted a privately mocking glance down at Jane. 'What can I say? It took four months before I could win her back.'

Sophie clapped her hands. 'Jane…you *are* the one for him. I knew it. No other woman would have run rings around him like that!'

Jane smiled weakly, wanting nothing more than to swing for Xavier, who was still clamping her to his side. They settled down to chat, Sophie clearly delighted to have another woman of similar standing on the island.

'It can get so boring sometimes…especially in the winter.' She winked at her husband cheekily. 'But now you're here we can do all sorts of things. Though you'll probably spend a lot of time on the mainland, with Xavier when he's working…'

Jane was quite happy to let her prattle on, horribly aware of Xavier's thigh pressed hard against her own on the small couch. What would they say if they knew that their marriage was a sham?

Before long they were in the hall, saying their goodbyes. Sophie embraced Jane. 'So don't forget the Winter Ball will be coming up next month. That calls for at least a few shopping trips… You lucky thing—at least it's in Xavier's hotel, your home from home.'

When they were gone, Jane turned to Xavier. 'How can you deceive your friends like that? Let them think that you're happily married?'

'What makes you think I'm not?'

Jane frowned at his obtuseness. 'But of course you're...
we're not. How can you say that?'

His eyes narrowed on her face, a shuttered look descending, making a chill run down her spine.

'Jane, I am very happily married, believe me. I've got the
most important thing I always wanted and expected to get out
of a marriage. An heir.'

She staved off the ice that settled around her heart at his
words. 'How can you be so cold?'

He smiled, but it didn't reach his eyes. 'You call me cold?
You're in this for your reasons too, or have you conveniently
forgotten them?'

A stillness came into the air around them. Nothing
moved; not a sound came from anywhere. She found her
voice and it sounded remarkably calm. 'No, I haven't. I'm
doing this for the baby. And I want my mother to be happy.
They are the only reasons I said yes. Certainly not for
anything else.'

Liar...

She felt her throat close over and wanted to get as far
away as possible right at that moment, but she forced herself
to stand strong.

He brought a large warm hand to her neck, caressing, and
the pulse thumped crazily against her skin and his. Every
muscle tensed as she fought against reacting, against closing
her eyes. When, oh, when would she be free of this debilitat-
ing desire for him?

'You'll never be free of me, Jane. You'll come to me.
Sooner or later. I'll wait. And until you do we will share our
bed. We both know you curled up in that tight ball beside me
to stop yourself reaching out and experiencing the passion
you know is still there.'

Her eyes widened as his words echoed her thoughts, as
if he had read her mind. Belatedly she remembered his
uncanny ability to do just that. But his arrogant assumption

helped to dampen her clamouring body. She tore his hand away from her neck.

'It's good to clarify things and know that at least we agree on our motivations for the marriage. It'll be a cold day in hell, Xavier, before we make love. I'm going for a walk.'

And she stormed out of the house, feeling as though the hounds of the Baskervilles were at her heels.

Xavier watched her go and felt rage surge upwards. He stormed into his study and poured himself a shot of whisky, gulping it back. His hand was a white-knuckle grip around the glass. How was she able to enrage him so? He'd never allowed any woman to affect him like this... How could she stand there so coolly and say those words?

A bleak expression crossed his face and he rubbed a weary hand over his eyes. It was nothing less than he'd said to her.

Why should it bother him that she felt exactly the same way? That she wasn't what he had imagined all those months ago? He had allowed himself to imagine for the first time ever something elusive, ethereal. A glimpse of fulfillment—what he saw Sophie and Paul share...he'd stupidly hoped that perhaps he too could have that sense of coming home...

He crushed the empty feeling. A foolish daydream, that was all it had been. He'd been wrong...it existed for others but not him. Never him.

A newly familiar surge of guilt rushed through him, and he swallowed back another shot to drown it out... Guilt was an emotion he had little time for. He conducted every aspect of his life with ruthless precision...so why should he feel guilt that maybe he...what? That he'd bullied her into marrying him? As she had just told him, she had her own very concrete reasons for entering the marriage. He shook his head. No way would she have given in unless she'd wanted to.

But she needed to...not wanted to. She told you she hated you for doing this to her, for not offering her another way...

He cursed the voice that mocked him.

It was just physical frustration. That was all. He'd never been denied a woman he desired before now. Her and her damned insistence that she didn't feel those *urges*. She hated the attraction. This was just her way of claiming control over the situation... The guilt rose again like a spectre. He swallowed another shot.

It had taken all the strength and will-power he possessed not to reach across the bed and pull her into his arms last night. Her achingly familiar sweet scent had tantalised his senses as he lay there, his body aroused to the point of pain, testing him beyond endurance. But he wouldn't do it...he couldn't. She was his *pregnant* wife, dammit. She would have to come to him.

When that day came...when she did come to him...maybe then that voice would disappear.

Another shot didn't help.

A few days later, a wan-faced Jane came into the dining room where Xavier was finishing breakfast. She eyed him warily. She'd had the most vivid dream last night. That he had pulled her close and tucked himself around her so completely that she'd felt unspeakably comforted, safe and cherished. She'd even felt love from it. And then she'd felt his hardness against her back, and it had started up a throbbing need that had woken her with its intensity. When she'd woken with a start, the bed had been empty. Xavier hadn't yet joined her, and the loneliness that had lodged in her chest had been so heavy that she still felt it this morning.

He looked at her over the rim of his coffee cup, and Jane hid her churning emotions behind a mask of bland happiness.

'Morning. Did you sleep well? Are you going to the mainland today? Isn't it lovely outside? I might go for a drive later, explore a bit.'

He frowned at her inane chatter, clearly not taken in.

'We're having some people over tonight—business colleagues, friends. A small dinner party. About ten people. Sophie and Paul, and Sasha will be there too. So you'll know a few.'

At the mention of Sasha's name, Jane nearly fell into her chair, her face paling. She'd managed to put the other woman out of her head, but now that awful morning came back vividly. Her own humiliation.

'Oh…that sounds nice.'

What else could she say? Don't you dare invite that woman?

'You'll act as hostess, of course.'

She just nodded her head. Still thinking about Sasha, distracted.

'I have to go to the hotel…I'll be back around seven p.m. The guests are due to arrive at eight.'

He drained the last of his coffee and got up to go. Just as he did Jane felt a flutter of something in her belly, and gasped audibly. Xavier came around to her side quickly.

'What is it? Is something wrong?'

Jane shook her head, her hand on her belly. 'I think I just felt the first kick.'

She turned to face him, smiling, her eyes gleaming with excitement. He crouched down beside her chair and she had the irresistible urge to reach out and take his hand, place it on her belly. The air around them grew heavy. She couldn't take her eyes from his. She saw his hand come out towards her, and suddenly checked herself. The feeling that he had read her mind was too strong, that he might have seen something on her face.

She flinched back. A tiny movement, but he saw it. His hand stopped. She saw his eyes harden. His face was inscrutable. A muscle twitched in his jaw.

'So you're all right.'

Jane gathered herself together. God, she was so transparent…she had to control these impulses.

She forced her voice to be light. 'Yes. It's nothing. It's probably not even the baby at all.'

She felt the acute disappointment that she couldn't share the moment with him. But she was far too vulnerable and weak in his presence; she had to maintain her guard at all times. Looking at him with welcoming eyes, wanting him to feel the baby move—that would have led her down a very dangerous path...

After helping Yvette and Jean-Paul prepare for the dinner, despite their remonstrations, Jane took a drive all the way up to the memorial at the other end of the island. It was bitter-sweet to be back there again and remember that day in the summer. She placed some flowers in the vases and lit a candle that was sheltered by the wind.

As she looked out to the sea, churning in a grey froth, she asked herself yet again what she was doing. Did she really have the strength to go through with this?

And then she felt the flutter again, barely perceptible, low in her abdomen. She turned and contemplated the view to the north. The view she had contemplated that day she'd come up here with Xavier, so full of optimism and joy, delighted expectation. And that night...that night was when this baby had been conceived. She unconsciously rubbed the bump beneath her jumper. That was why she was here. Loving Xavier was unfortunate, incidental, and not giving in to his potent seductiveness was her main priority. She had to remember that.

She was dressed and ready that evening when Xavier returned. His sharp, assessing eyes took her in. A long indolent look up and down that left her breathing faster. She cursed his ability to weaken her.

'Very nice.'

'Thank you,' she answered tightly.

She had tied her hair back in a loose knot, and was wearing a midnight-blue silk button-down dress. Demure and classic.

He reached into his pocket and pulled out a small box, handing it to her. She looked from him to it, a small frown creasing her forehead as she took it. When she opened it she had to hold back a gasp. Sapphire drop earrings glistened against the velvet background. They were stunning. Priceless. Her eyes flew up to his.

'But…what's this for? I can't take these; they're far too expensive.'

His voice was almost harsh, his face closed. 'Just take them, Jane. I got them to match your ring… You'll be getting plenty more jewels in time, and I'll expect you to wear them.'

Of course he would. She had a certain standard to maintain, didn't she? As his wife, she would be expected to wear jewels, compete with the other women in their society. The rush of pleasure she had felt initially at receiving such a gift was quashed.

As he'd said, they were to match her ring. He hadn't put any more thought into it apart from that.

She could be just as closed. She took them out of the box and put them in her ears, feeling as though they were piercing her heart, not the lobes of her ears. They felt heavy. She handed him back the box.

'Thank you for the gift. Excuse me. I have to help Yvette get the dining room ready.'

And with a straight back she walked away, barely hearing him take the stairs two at a time.

Jane threw herself into helping get the dining room ready to take her mind off their exchange, and it was just before the guests were due to arrive that Xavier appeared again downstairs. She was putting the finishing touches to a vase of flowers she'd picked herself on her excursion earlier, and looked up, her hands stilling of their own accord as she took him in.

He wasn't formally dressed, but had changed into a dark grey suit and a snowy white shirt with the top button open, giving a tantalising glimpse of dark skin and hair just underneath. Jane could almost feel the heat emanating from his chest as he paused on the bottom step. He took her breath away. Literally. Cleanshaven, hair swept back, sardonic eyes taking her in.

She burned up with colour at how she'd been caught staring to intently. Had she lost her mind? She was meant to be keeping him at arm's length, not drooling over him—and certainly not so obviously.

'Still blushing, Jane...? How remarkably sweet.'

Before she could answer, the doorbell pealed and Xavier took her arm.

'Time to act the loving wife.'

She smiled her way through the introductions as everyone seemed to arrive at once—Sasha being the last. She came in and threw her arms around Xavier's neck, pressing an eager kiss to his cheek. Jane couldn't take her eyes off the display, the way Sasha looked so sexy draped in his arms, blonde contrasting with dark. Xavier caught her eye and pulled himself out of Sasha's arms.

'Sasha, you remember Jane...my wife?'

Was there a subtle possessive inflection there? Jane wondered. Or was it just wishful thinking on her part?

'Sasha, how nice to see you again,' she said, lying through her teeth. 'Please come through. What would you like to drink?'

Sasha avoided Jane's eye, clinging on to Xavier's arm as they went into the main drawing room, where the rest of the guests were enjoying their aperitifs.

By the time they were on coffee and desserts, Jane's cheeks ached from smiling. Thankfully Sasha was at the other end of the table, beside Sophie, who had thrown Jane a few pained looks during dinner. At least now she didn't feel as though her dislike of Sasha was just in her own head.

Back in the drawing room afterwards, she rested on the arm of a chair, talking to the very friendly wife of one of

Xavier's older colleagues. She felt a prickle of awareness, and looked up to catch him staring at her from across the room.

The weight and intensity of his gaze caught her by surprise and, not having the time to react and school her features, she felt her body responding to his look, crying out for fulfilment. Her breasts grew heavy, and she felt her nipples harden into tight points, and that treacherous all-revealing flush stain her cheeks. She was unable to tear her gaze away from his, as if he'd put some kind of spell on her.

Sophie finally broke it, when she rolled her eyes and said to the room at large, 'Newlyweds! What is it the Americans say? Oh, yes! Get a room! We didn't come here to see you two devour each other with looks.'

Everyone laughed, and Jane blushed even harder. How had she ever thought she could handle this enforced celibacy?

And it was about to get worse.

Xavier, taking full advantage of the situation, strolled over and caught Jane up to him with one graceful move. He bent his head, taking her mouth with such a sweet kiss that a wave of longing made her shudder in his arms. His action was so swift that he took her off guard, much as he had with his look.

When he pulled away, her mouth clung to his, reluctant to let him go, and with a dazed look she realised that they were still in the room, and it hadn't been some dream. She couldn't let go of the feeling that had surged through her body, every point sensitive to his touch, his presence…the sheer sexiness of it, her breasts crushed against him.

She looked into his eyes and saw them flicker around the room. Reality crashed around her. An act…that was all it was. An act to unnerve her and for the guests.

She spoke quickly to hide her vulnerability, afraid he might read something into her easy acquiescence. 'I hope that was convincing enough for you?'

When she tried to pull out of his arms, they tightened. His

eyes flashed down at her. 'If I'd known you were going to be so happy to comply and act along then I'd have taken advantage a lot sooner…but rest assured I'll remember next time.'

And with a casual kiss on her wrist, he calmly strolled back to the other side of the room.

Xavier watched Jane from under hooded lids. She was studiously avoiding looking anywhere near him. He was only half taking in Paul's conversation, glad that there was a third person so he could watch her without appearing rude.

The kiss had unsettled him. How quickly he'd become aroused, likc a flash fire. Rapidly devouring any sense of reality except what he felt when he touched her. He had felt how ripe and lush she was, more curved, rounded. The feel of her belly, pressing low against his groin… The intense possessiveness he'd felt had nearly floored him…she was *his* woman…carrying *his* baby. The thought of other men looking at her blooming beauty, the burgeoning curves, made his hands curl into fists.

Only registering the presence of their guests had held him back from hauling her up into his arms and out of the room…much like the caveman impulse he'd felt when he'd first brought her into this house. Amazingly, after all this time, he still felt the same out-of-control desire—if anything it had grown even stronger, and with it he felt…weak. Like Samson and Delilah, he thought with a small hard smile to himself. As if she was sucking his strength. Taking his power.

He could see how her chest rose and fell with uneven breaths, the V of her dress giving tantalising glimpses of her breasts, which pushed against the silk. He'd felt them through the fabric of their clothes. He wondered if they looked different now she was pregnant. Were they already fuller, harder?

His erection grew again, and he shifted uncomfortably. Then he remembered that morning, in the breakfast room.

When she'd turned that innocent gaze on him, so full of delight at the joy of their baby. Her hand on her belly, feeling something that he could only imagine. He'd ached with the sudden need to reach out and share what she was feeling, share the experience, and he had been sure the invitation had been in her eyes, her face. But then…just when he'd reached out…she'd flinched back, and the icy cool look had come down. Something inside him had shriveled up. He had done that to her. She could barely bring herself to look at him.

That the baby could bring such effortless joy to her face but not him… He resolutely turned away from her and back to the conversation, a heavy feeling in his heart. A place he'd never given much thought to…until now.

Finally the last guests left, and Jane closed the door wearily. She'd told Yvette and Jean-Paul to go to bed long ago. Thank God that was over. She rubbed a hand over her tired eyes and pulled her hair free at the back of her head, massaging her scalp.

Xavier stood in the doorway of the drawing room. 'Care for a nightcap? Non-alcoholic, of course,' he added dryly.

She had a sudden overwhelming urge to walk over, run her hands under his jacket, lean into his tall body and say, *Take me to bed. Make love to me until we can't move any more.*

As if that scenario existed in some parallel world. A world where he loved her as much as she loved him.

But it didn't. She quashed the seductive daydream and instead moved towards the stairs, every cell in her body screaming to go in the other direction.

'No, thanks. I'm tired.'

'Of course. Wouldn't want you to miss out on any sleep. It mightn't be good for the baby.'

She looked at him warily as she got to the bottom step, saw him tip his glass back and drain the contents with something savage in his movements.

'Goodnight.' And she fled.

CHAPTER TWELVE

A MONTH later Jane was getting ready for the Winter Ball, which was that evening. Her hands shook as she put earrings in her ears, smoothed back her hair and flicked some lint off her dress.

Her nerves were wound so tightly now that she jumped at the slightest sound or movement. The last few weeks had been an exercise in torture. Self-inflicted torture. On the outside she was the picture of a glowing pregnancy. The sleepless nights, waking with muscles cramping from tension, hadn't yet told on her face, apart from faint dark circles. Xavier hadn't touched her again since that devastating kiss in front of their guests, but she could hardly look at him for fear of him seeing the naked desire on her face. She avoided him whenever she could. Slept late or got up early. Whatever was required.

He spent some nights on the mainland, and those were the only ones she slept. On a rational level she welcomed this, but on every other *honest* level she missed his presence with a physical pain that was almost unbearable. One day he'd brushed past her, barely touched her, and it had caused such an intense spiking of desire to rush through her that she'd had to restrain herself from grabbing him.

That was just what he wanted. Her to give in, beg him for release.

And…in weak moments…she had begun to entertain treacherous thoughts of doing just that. But each time she did, she'd remember why she couldn't... What if she couldn't keep her feelings hidden?

She sighed loudly in the empty room, and turned side-on to check her reflection. She smoothed the black empire line dress over her bump. It was growing every day, still neat, but now very evident.

A sound made her jump. Xavier stood against the doorjamb nonchalantly, devastating in a tuxedo. A memory of the first time she had seen him like that, by the pool in the hotel, came rushing back with such sudden force that she felt faint, and grabbed on to the table beside her to stay steady.

In two quick strides he was by her side, a hand curling around her arm.

'What is it?'

She shook her head, warding him off. 'No...nothing. Just a dizzy moment. I'm fine.'

He dropped his grip as though burnt, and ran an angry hand through his immaculate hair, leaving it tousled. 'For pity's sake, Jane, would you expect me to leave you lying there if you'd collapsed? I haven't laid a hand on you in weeks. Your startled jumps and fearful glances aren't exactly arousing me to passionate heights.'

He was furious, his pulse beating erratically against the skin of his neck. And all she wanted to do was reach out and press her lips against it. Feel the flutter under her mouth, taste his skin, see if it still had that musky tang...

She closed her eyes. 'I'm sorry. Of course I don't expect you to jump on me.'

The way she was feeling, she was more likely to jump on him.

She was a mess. A mass of churning frustrated emotions and desires...he was the cool one.

'The helicopter is ready; the Jeep is waiting. I'll be downstairs.'

He left the room.

Jane turned back to the mirror. Noticed her cheeks burning up, the fever-bright glitter of her eyes. Her breasts pushing against the fabric of the dress felt heavy and full. It was herself she needed protection from, not him. She closed her eyes at her reflection in despair.

By the time they got to the hotel she was calm again. Relatively. It was her first time back there since returning to France, and the memories rushing up were kept down with difficulty. She'd had plenty of opportunity to go to the mainland before now—Sophie rang nearly every other day to check in and ask her out—but Jane kept begging off. Somehow she knew she wouldn't be able to cope with Sophie's easy friendliness. She was just holding it together for herself. The island had become something of a sanctuary.

She followed Xavier to the main ballroom. He stopped her just before entering, the muted sounds of an orchestra coming from behind the doors.

'Ready for the performance of your life?' he drawled.

She nodded jerkily, avoiding his eye. She suddenly felt exhausted, as though she was conducting an impossible immense uphill battle.

'I am if you are.'

'Oh, I've been ready for some time.'

She ignored the implication in his tone. He took her hand in his and led her into the huge main ballroom, the crowd and sounds stunning Jane for a second after the peace of the island.

She nodded and smiled her way through the crush. With the help of Yvette she'd been picking up more and more French, and was now able to converse haltingly at Xavier's side.

A couple of hours later, after speeches and auctions in aid of charity, Jane was trapped by a very boring colleague of Xavier's. Some sixth sense made her realise that they'd become separated. She looked around and found him on the other side of the room. It wasn't hard. He stood head and shoulders above everyone else. His dark head was inclined towards someone. Jane couldn't see who, but then the crowd cleared and she had an unimpeded view. It was Sasha, in a stunning cream backless gown that showed off a smooth, tanned expanse of bare back. She was holding Xavier's arm, her head thrown back, throat exposed, laughing at something he'd just said.

Jane felt a red-hot poker right through her heart, and shook with the desire to march over there and rip every tousled blonde lock out one by one.

'She's a piece of work, isn't she?'

She looked around suddenly, aware that her heart was racing and shocked at the intensity of her feelings. To her relief she saw that the man had gone and Sophie was beside her.

They kissed each other's cheeks in greeting. Jane tried to make sense of her comment.

'What do you mean…piece of work?'

Sophie nodded her head towards Xavier and Sasha.

Jane feigned uninterest. 'Oh, that…'

Sophie flicked her hand in a very gallic gesture. 'Sasha…she's nothing. No, my dear. The women you need to watch out for are the ones giving you dagger looks.'

'What?' Jane followed Sophie's gaze and saw all the beautiful women dotted around the room, and she did indeed catch some looks that were none too friendly.

'Who…who are they?'

'They're the ones who thought they had a chance, who want to be where you are—married to Xavier and expecting his child.'

Sophie caught her husband gesturing at her from across the room and winked at Jane, 'My man wants me… I know what you might think, chérie, but you're quite welcome to your Alpha man…I'll take my pot-bellied version any day!'

Jane had to laugh at Sophie's outrageous sense of humour as she disappeared into the crowd.

Her smile faded, though, as she took in the women who had just been pointed out. More than a few speculative looks *were* coming her way, and she suddenly imagined them all shooting come-hither looks to Xavier.

She felt a huge surge of possessiveness and jealousy. So strong that she shook with it. Her first time out in public with her husband and she wanted to rip the head off every woman in a ten-mile radius. This didn't bode well.

She looked across the room again. Sasha had now been joined by two other beauties. They surrounded Xavier. Vying for his attention. A cold rage filled her body. Acting purely on some primeval instinct she was barely aware of, she started to walk over to him, not even thinking about what she would do when she got there.

She kept getting bumped and jostled by the crowd. Suddenly a tall man appeared in front of her, didn't move. She looked up…for a second her brain stopped working and then cleared.

'I don't believe it…Pete?'

'Jane!'

She kissed him on his cheek. 'You're still here! It's so lovely to see you…'

It all rushed back—her blind date with Pete, the night she'd met Xavier properly for the first time. She remembered his easy, unthreatening presence, and it was like a soothing balm to her soul. She smiled up at him widely.

'I was due to return home in September, but I met someone just before I did…and decided to stay on.' He blushed endearingly. 'We're getting married in the spring.'

'Oh, Pete, I'm so happy for you. That's wonderful news.'

Impulsively she reached up to kiss him again, a silly jealous dart rising unbidden at his exuberant happiness. When she stepped back, he had a funny look on his face.

Jane frowned. 'What…what's wrong?'

But she knew. She felt the familiar prickle of awareness.

An arm snaked around her waist, holding her firm. Xavier held out a hand to Pete. Jane could feel the tension radiating off him in waves.

'I'm Jane's husband…and you are?'

Pete visibly swallowed. 'Pete Sullivan.'

Jane couldn't believe Xavier was being so rude. Pete mumbled something and made a quick escape—Jane barely had a chance to say goodbye properly. She rounded on Xavier, pulling herself out of his embrace, but he had other ideas. He clamped a hand around hers and pulled her into an alcove where they were hidden from the room.

'Who the hell was *that*?' he snarled.

'Well, if you'd been acting like a human being I could have introduced you properly.'

'You were all over him.'

'Hardly, Xavier.'

'Well?'

She crossed her arms in front of her chest. 'I'm not going to dignify your behaviour with an explanation.'

'Oh, yes, you are…' A funny look came into his eyes. She recognised that darkening, that intent as he bent towards her, and instinctively pulled back, her hands coming up.

'Xavier…no.'

Hard hands took her arms. 'Yes, Jane. If you can kiss perfect strangers in front of the whole room, then you can kiss your damn husband.'

'He's not a stranger!' she cried desperately.

It was the worst thing she could have said. All she had was a glimpse of flashing green before the light was blocked and Xavier's mouth slanted over hers.

Her drew her in close to his body and kissed her with raw, unchecked passion. She tried not to respond, but her hands weren't obeying the order to push away…they rested between them, ineffectual.

The fire that had been simmering for weeks turned into an inferno…and on a deep sigh, she gave in. It was too strong for her to fight. And she was so tired of fighting it.

When he realised she wasn't resisting him, his arms relaxed and one hand moved to cup her bottom through the silk of her dress. The other threaded through soft hair, tilting her head, allowing his tongue to delve deeper.

Her hands uncurled and with sweet hesitancy climbed up his chest, until they were around his neck, holding him tight. She traced his lips with her tongue, her breath coming in short, sharp gasps, fingers tangling in the silky strands of hair that curled over his collar. He didn't allow her any quarter. His hand moved up, skimming, touching her more rounded curves, over her belly and up, until she felt him cup the heavy weight of her breast.

She'd never felt as womanly, as desirable. She tore her mouth away with a moan as his thumb found a jutting nipple and flicked it through her dress. With her increased sensitivity everywhere, it nearly pushed her over the edge.

His head dipped and he took her mouth again, remorseless, until Jane was weak and clinging to him with a powerful desire pulsing through her entire trembling body.

He finally tore his mouth away, both of them breathing hard.

She pulled back, and this time he let her go. Through the haze of desire that pounded in her blood, Jane couldn't believe she'd let him kiss her like that. Or that she'd kissed him back. All of her precious barriers, so carefully in place to guard her weak heart. Torn down with a kiss. And it was blatantly obvious that her so-called *urges* were very much there.

She shook her head dumbly, suddenly remembering seeing him surrounded by that bevy of beauties. He was just staking his claim. On his property. In case she was getting any ideas.

Xavier looked at her, colour high on his cheeks, his lips curled derisively. 'Don't look at me like that, Jane…you wanted it as much as I did.'

She turned quickly and half-ran, half-walked back through the room, praying that he wasn't following. She muttered apologies as she crashed into people, unseeing. All she wanted was to get out of there. Suddenly she felt more claustrophobic than she'd ever been in her life.

Finally she stumbled out into the lobby on unsteady legs, breathing hard. Xavier was right behind her. She backed away.

'Xavier, please leave me alone.'

'Jane, you were with me back there every step of the way…you were very responsive.'

So responsive, in fact, that his body tightened again just at the thought.

Her eyes flashed and the possessive rage coursed through her again. 'Only half as responsive, I'm sure, as Sasha…or any of the other willing ladies in there.'

Someone walked out of the room and Xavier grabbed Jane's elbow, leading her to a quiet corner.

'What are you talking about?'

'I'd like to know exactly what is going on with you and Sasha.' Fire spat from her eyes.

He frowned for a second. 'What on earth do you mean?'

'I saw you with her…it didn't exactly look innocent. Every time she sees you she jumps all over you, and hisses at me like a cat.'

And what about the other women?

He took her shoulders and she tried to break free, but he wouldn't let her. 'I've known Sasha since she was a baby. She's had a crush on me for years…a stupid crush.'

He paused and looked at her assessingly, dangerously.

'Jealous, Jane? You won't let me touch you, but can't stand the thought of other women?'

She snorted, hiding the panic. *What was she thinking?*

'Hardly…don't flatter yourself.'

But the words sounded weak to her ears. She tried to evade

his gaze, but it was impossible. She realised that what he said was true. She didn't want those other women near him with a passion that scared her.

His hands tightened. 'Who was he?'

She looked up, feeling sudden relief that his attention had been taken from her disastrous admission of jealousy, from her raw emotions.

'Pete?'

Jane could feel him barely reining his temper in. His heavy-lidded gaze bored into her.

'Yes…who is he?'

She contemplated not answering him, but knew it was futile. And she certainly didn't want him focusing on her reaction to Sasha again.

'I met him the night I came here for dinner after the day trip. He was my blind date… He's living here, working in town. He was just telling me about the girl he's getting married to.' She looked into his eyes, something twisting in her heart. 'What a coincidence, both of us finding our true loves here…'

Her sarcastic comment bounced off him. She could see his rapier-sharp mind make the connection, recognition drop. He straightened up to his full intimidating height and let her go. She swayed precariously. It was all too much…the crowds, the other women, Sasha, the kiss…and underneath it all this all-consuming, still raging desire for this man who just wanted her for the baby in her belly.

She felt herself being lifted against his chest and closed her eyes, a blessed numbness taking over. Felt herself being carried through a door and then carefully put down. She realised she was sitting on the edge of the bed in the penthouse suite.

Xavier was at her feet, taking off her shoes. 'What are you doing?'

He shot her a quelling look. 'Relax, Jane. You're obviously exhausted; you need to rest. Lie down for a while and I'll come back to check on you.'

He pushed her down onto the bed and drew a cover over her in the darkened room.

But then, instead of moving, he rested on his hands over her for a timeless moment. Jane looked up, transfixed by his eyes. It was as if time stood still. She saw something in the green depths, some expression of desire and blatant need that connected with the deepest part of her so strongly that she felt energy course through her system, exhaustion forgotten.

Xavier closed his eyes for a split second. She could see the pulse throb in his temple. Then he stood and straightened, looking down from his great height. Distant and remote, he stepped away from her.

He opened the door, about to walk out, and stopped. Jane's breath stopped too. He shut the door again and rested his hands on it, his head bent. Then he turned around with a sudden savage movement and strode back towards the bed, taking off his jacket as he did so. Jane's eyes widened, the breath coming jerkily in and out of her mouth as he came back and leant over her on his arms.

'Xavier…what are you…?' Her hands came up automatically between them when she saw the feral glitter in his eyes. He kept coming down, closer and closer. Her hands tried to push but he was immovable. She could feel her blood throbbing through her body, that energy pulsing through every cell.

'I want to sleep with my wife…I've waited long enough, and after that kiss…' His mouth tightened. 'God, Jane, how can you deny us this?'

He came closer, his torso practically touching her chest. She could feel her breasts swell against her dress, the nipples peaking into hard points. Her hands still pushed ineffectually at the hard wall of muscle.

Closer and closer.

She shut her eyes as she felt his mouth near her ear, his lips a breath away from touching. She was trembling all over.

'If you push very, very hard, push me away, I'll go back downstairs and leave you alone. But know this. I need you, Jane. I want you so much it hurts.'

His words resounded and echoed in her, through her. She hurt too. All over. The heat from his chest enveloped her, his scent arousing her beyond anything she'd ever felt. But she couldn't do this...had to resist. She pushed. Nothing. He didn't budge. Pushed again, harder.

Xavier expelled a harsh breath and started to pull away. Suddenly Jane had a vision of him walking out through the door, back downstairs to all those predatory women. Saw an aching lonely void when he left the room. It was the same as the kiss—she was suddenly tired, so tired of fighting herself, him...*this*.

Her hands stopped pushing. He stopped. She looked into his eyes and knew with fatal clarity that she could not let him walk out. She needed him with an aching, craving desire that obliterated all coherent thought and washed through her with such force that she shook.

Her hands moved up and around his neck. She pulled his head back to her.

On a mutual sigh of relief his arms came around her tightly and his tongue entered her mouth with one igniting stroke that mimicked another form of penetration so vividly that Jane moaned deep in her throat, her tongue meeting his, melding and mating and dancing.

She couldn't think beyond the here and now. She was too far gone. She'd worry about it later. Their kiss quickly got out of control as her hands roved over his chest, back, wherever she could reach. It was heaven to be able to finally touch him...and she wanted him to touch her...all over.

He drew back, breathing harshly, and pulled her up to a sitting position. His hands ran over her shoulders, glanced down over breasts that ached against the confines of her clothes.

'Take it off. I need to see you...'

She pulled the dress over her head awkwardly, feeling suddenly shy. She hadn't been naked before him since the summer. Xavier gazed at her wonderingly, a hand reaching out to cup her breast. They strained against the lace cups of her bra, bigger, the veins visible under the translucent skin, and then his hand moved down to her belly, the proud hard swell. He bent his head and pressed a kiss to the skin, his hand visibly shaking as he traced the smooth contour. She felt immeasurably moved.

He flicked open the front clasp of her bra, letting her breasts tumble free. The clamouring of her pulse got louder and she sucked in a hard breath, her head thrown back as his hot mouth bent and suckled there. A throbbing heat pulsed between her legs.

'You…I need to see you too,' she muttered thickly, coming up on her knees to pull off his bow tie, and open his shirt, her hands trembling. A button popped, and then she was smoothing it off his shoulders, baring him to her hungry gaze. How had she survived till now without this?

He sat back for a moment, watched as she bent forward, pressed her mouth against his skin, found a hard flat nipple, nipped gently. His hand threaded through her hair, holding her head, and she heard the whistle of his sucked-in breath.

Hands on her shoulders, gently he put her away from him, and she watched with a dry mouth as he stood and kicked off the rest of his clothes.

His body was even more beautiful than she remembered. The long lean lines, every muscle and sinew taut, the warm olive gleam of his skin rippling as he stepped back to the bed. Her gaze travelled down and her pulse ratcheted up a few notches when she saw his erection. It was bigger and harder than she remembered, and she felt a liquid burst of desire in response.

He caught her look and said wryly, 'It's been a while.'

He must mean since getting married, Jane thought dimly.

And then couldn't think as he took her shoulders and pressed her back down onto the bed. He rested over her on strong arms, the muscles bunching. She reached up, revelling in the feel of him, the satin warm skin, the musky scent. The strength of his body poised over hers made her quake with the need to take him into her, know him again.

His mouth was hot on her neck, on her pulse, beating out of control. He rested on his elbows over her, careful to keep her shielded from his full weight. She could feel the entire length of his body against her, his hardness against her belly. She writhed in response, a small moan escaping when his hair roughened chest stimulated her breasts unbearably.

He pulled back slightly, brought a hand up to skim over her shoulders, down over her breasts, before his mouth dropped and paid homage to each hard thrusting peak in turn. She was not herself any more. She sucked in jerky breaths, arching against him. His breath tickled as his mouth finally moved down, over her belly and lower, where she felt his fingers hook around her panties and pull them down, stockings following.

When she was naked, he pulled her into his body, torso to torso, legs entwined around hers, every part of their bodies touching. Jane could feel the tremors run through her. It was too much, too heady after so long…her breathing was laboured. She needed him, wanted him so badly.

He spoke her thoughts out loud. 'I don't think I can wait…or go slowly…'

'Me neither…' She arched as his hand caressed between her legs, fingers finding the moist centre of her desire. Stroking back and forth.

'You're so ready.'

She was half crazed with the need to feel him inside her, and instinctively lifted her leg over his hip, bringing her into intimate contact with his erection. It jumped and pulsed against her body. Xavier moved down slightly, keeping her leg lifted, and with one smooth thrust entered her. Jane cried out with the sensation, her walls tight around him after all this time.

'Have I hurt you?'

He went to withdraw and Jane grabbed him. 'No…don't stop.'

He started to thrust upwards, one arm around her back holding her steady, the other on her leg, holding it over his hip. And all the time came that delicious building, tightening, as they climbed and climbed, his strokes going deeper, harder, filling her exquisitely. She blindly sought his mouth and kissed him, unable to contain her instinctive drives any more. She arched towards him and felt every part of herself clench as with one last thrust Xavier sent her into a huge explosion of stars that left her quivering around his body just as he joined her in his own climax. She felt his power spill into her, deep in her body.

It was unbearably, exquisitely intimate, lying like this, still joined, face to face, their breath mingling, every inch of skin in contact, legs entwined.

When they were finally breathing normally Xavier shifted himself free of Jane's embrace, causing her to gasp again, her body still painfully sensitive.

He turned her gently, so her back was tucked into his chest, pulled a sheet over their bodies and pressed a kiss to the back of her head. A heavy, possessive arm lay around the swell of her belly, a hand stretched out to cover it.

She felt a kick in her belly under Xavier's hand and stilled.

'Did you feel that?'

It came again, stronger, and she turned a shining happy face up to him, holding his hand firm against her belly. 'Oh, Xavier, did you feel that?'

As he looked down into her face and felt the baby kick, he felt something inside him close off. Shut down.

He had to get away. Now… He couldn't trust himself here with her. He felt raw, exposed. They had just shared the strongest climax he could ever remember experiencing, and he'd been pretty sure it was the same for her, and yet…it was the baby that was giving her that glow of happiness, that smile as she looked up into his face.

Images and sensations rushed through him…the red mist of anger that had settled over his vision when he'd seen her talking to Pete…the feel of the baby kicking under her smooth skin…her happiness for that but not him—and the fear. The fear that he was falling into some place that he'd never find his way out of again…

She was just giving in to carnal desires—desires she had been resisting. She'd almost pushed him away; he'd almost left the room. It was laughable. Instead of the mocking voice in his head stopping, now it was all he could hear. He had to get out.

Jane felt the tension in Xavier's body, tried to gauge the look on his face.

He pulled his hand away from under hers and pulled himself out of the bed. She drew the sheet up over her chest, feeling a sudden chill. Xavier was stepping back into his clothes, a million miles away from the man who had just tucked her into his body. A cold look of detachment on his face, the angles harsh in the dim light.

'I should go back downstairs in case we're missed.'

He picked up his jacket and cast her a quick glance as he left the room.

'I'm glad you've decided it's time to be my wife. *Properly.*'

CHAPTER THIRTEEN

JANE lay in the bed, tucked into a curled-up position, for some time. Until the air began to chill her skin and she had to pull another blanket onto the bed to stop her teeth chattering.

This was exactly what she had feared. Sleeping with him had opened her up, taken the scab off the wound…and now she was afraid there would be no way to stem the flow of blood. This intimacy had cracked her heart open completely. And there was no going back. No closing it off again. After this…she couldn't.

What had she done…?

The next morning when she woke she was in the bed alone, and knew that Xavier hadn't joined her at all. Her body ached with a betrayingly pleasurable ache as she got up and belted a robe firmly around her waist. When she went out into the suite she paled visibly when she saw him standing at the window, pristine in a dark suit. He ran a cool look over her as she emerged, feeling sleepy and tousled in comparison. Her heart hardened when she saw the lack of anything on his face.

'Morning.'

'Morning.'

'I have to go to Paris for a couple of days…something's come up.'

She exuded what she hoped was an air of extreme uninterest, fighting the reaction of her body to the musky scent
that reached her nostrils, the smell of which was bringing last
night back to vivid life. Her voice sounded strained to her
ears.

'Fine…I'll go back to the island later on. Sophie said
something about meeting for lunch, so I might do that.'

Xavier was very still as Jane helped herself to coffee and
a croissant. She moved over towards a chair at the other end
of the table and had to walk past him. He blocked her way,
and she nearly jumped out of her skin. He took the cup and
plate out of her hand and put his hands on her arms. She carefully schooled her features before looking up, but started
trembling when she took in the green eyes, smoky like last
night, took in his mouth and quickly returned to his eyes. His
mouth was far too potent.

'Jane…no more of the startled rabbit. We can't go back
after last night.'

He took his hands away and ran one through his hair impatiently. 'Hell, Jane, you stopped pushing me away. I
almost left…'

Every self-protective mechanism kicked in. She shrugged
negligently. 'It's no big deal, Xavier. I'm quite aware of what
I did. We both got what we wanted.'

A hand came to her jaw, forcing her face up to his. She
flinched inwardly at the hardness in his face. The lack of
emotion.

*The voice in his head would stop. He'd make it…and this
was how.*

'Good. Because when I get back we are going to be man
and wife…properly…from now on.'

Jane refused to give in to the desire to run as fast as she
could, stood her ground. She had got herself into this and
there was no way that he would ever know how much it was
going to kill her to be intimate, how much she feared her heart

was going to break with every encounter, every time he left her so dispassionately afterwards.

Why, oh, why had she been so weak? She'd hit the self-destruct button. Spectacularly. And she couldn't even blame him! As he had pointed out, she had pulled him back to her, had made the choice.

Xavier held her jaw in a light but firm grip and bent his head, his breath tickling her face for a moment before he touched his mouth to hers. Even now, despite her pain, the pull was too strong, the desire overwhelming to just sink against his body, pull him close, allow him full access.

'I'll see you in two days…'

Two days later, back in the castle, Jane was like a cat on a hot tin roof. Listening out for the helicopter or the Jeep. Trying to read and giving up. Watching the TV and giving up. She knew she was irritating Yvette by getting under her feet, and took herself out for a walk to burn off the excess energy.

As much as she dreaded seeing Xavier again, she hungered for him now in a way she never had before. She had convinced herself in the past two days that she could do this…maintain a physical relationship and keep her feelings back. She couldn't fight him again. If she did, that razor-sharp mind would focus on her motivations and not let go until he'd found the beating heart of her.

And that weak heart, so brimming over with love for him, was what she had to guard against. She had nearly revealed it that night, when she'd felt the baby kick. And that was what had driven him from the bed. She was sure of it. She had seen the dawning horror on his face, the cool detachment as he had firmly extricated himself from her embrace.

She wouldn't make that mistake again.

When she returned to the castle there was still no sign of him. She tried not to worry, and picked up the phone countless times only to put it down again. He'd love that, wouldn't he? No doubt he'd laugh at her attempt to be a concerned wife. But the truth was she *was* concerned. She paced back and forth in the sitting room, looking out of the window at the skies that looked ominously grey.

Yvette appeared at the door, an indulgent smile on her face. '*Madame*, don't worry…he will be here. You should go to bed.'

Jane smiled weakly and nodded. 'Maybe you're right.'

It was a relief not to have to hold back her feelings with the other woman. Yvette assumed, of course, that Jane was madly in love.

She climbed the stairs and once in bed eventually fell asleep, despite the niggling worry.

Xavier walked into the bedroom, every bone and muscle in his body screaming with fatigue. Two days of intense negotiations and then he had flown himself back to the island on the plane. Ordinarily he would have stayed overnight in Paris. He had never had the overwhelming desire to come home before…

But now he did. And the reason was curled up under the covers. Her hair was fanned out on the pillow, lashes long against her cheek, and he could imagine the hidden curves. Her arms were bare and his body hardened in an instant at the thought of her naked.

He stripped and got into the bed, pulling her body close into his, breathing in her sweet scent. He felt the flimsy silk of her slip. She'd never worn this before…was it because she'd been waiting for him? The thought made him harder. His hand was firm on her belly, just under the weight of her breasts, and he cupped one full heavy mound, delighting in the way her nipple sprang to hard life in his palm.

He couldn't shut out the thought: She might want this for now…but you know she would resist if she could…she's going to hate you for this…sooner or later…

He blocked it out with every ounce of will-power, pushed it into some dark recess. It was too heady…too seductive… being here, having her in his arms like this…

Jane was half asleep and moaned softly in her drowsy state. She couldn't believe it. She was having that dream again. When would it stop?

She wiggled to try and force herself to wake up, but instead of the feelings subsiding as she became more awake, they got stronger. The pulse beating between her legs was all too real, as was the hand on her breast, the nudging of a very aroused man low at her back.

She came to full tense alertness. Her head falling back. 'Xavier…'

His mouth was busy trailing a hot blaze of fire down the back of her neck. Relief coursed through her. She tried to stay coherent for a moment, not in this all too dangerous dream-like state where anything could happen, anything might be said…

'Xavier…where were you?'

He lifted his head and she could just make out the glittering green in the darkness. His voice was sardonic, but didn't quench her desire, which was fast spiralling out of control.

'You missed me…?'

She blustered, 'No, of course not.'

He was pulling up her silk slip, up over her thighs. She hesitated for a split second and then lifted them to help, and felt his moan of approval against her back as he slipped her free of the flimsy garment entirely with one swift move.

Had she somehow subconsciously picked it because, if she was honest, she'd imagined this very scenario…?

She turned her head so that her lips were close to his. His mouth hovered over them for an infinitesimal moment and then he took them with a drugging, heated kiss, his tongue invading, exploring, plundering her weak, non-existent defence.

His hands on her breasts roused them to hard, engorged

points, and she gasped when he took his mouth away from hers. Keeping her back to him, he brought an arm under one leg, lifting it slightly, opening her up for him to explore with long fingers, feel the telling wetness, arousing her to even further heights.

She bit her lip to stop from crying out as she felt him guide his hard length into her tight passage, his chest pressed close against her, his hand holding her in place as he smoothly thrust in and out.

She was fast being borne away in an ever tightening need, the eroticism of the position, the hunger with which they both sought to reach the pinnacle, something almost animalistic in their movements helping them to reach a simultaneous climax of such strength that Jane felt everything go black for a split second…and then came back down on the shuddering waves of her orgasm, her body clenching and pulsating around Xavier for long moments.

How was it that they could reach this intoxicating peak every time without love? Words trembled on her lips. She turned her head and blindly sought his mouth…every buried wish and desire naked for him to see…if only he could.

Then she tensed abruptly. This was what she had to fight. This uncontrollable awful need to blurt out her feelings.

Xavier felt her distancing herself and pulled free from her body. He needed no further indication. They had scratched their itch.

He lay on his back by her side, and didn't pull her into his arms as she curled away from him. Jane lay for a long time staring into the dark. Long after Xavier had turned away on the opposite side and his breathing had slowed and deepened.

Two weeks later…two long weeks of similar nights…nights of blinding, all-consuming passion followed by each of them turning away from the other…Jane walked into the dining room, the toll now obvious on her face. Dark circles were evident under her eyes, and no amount of make-up could disguise the puffiness. She knew she couldn't keep going on like this. Despite her grand justifications to herself. She had hit the wall of as much emotional pain she could take.

Xavier took in her appearance with a sharp look.

'You don't look well.'

She bristled at his tone. He didn't have to point out to her what she knew herself. The bloom had gone. In the past few days she had even begun feeling nauseous again.

'It's called being pregnant, Xavier. I'm sorry, but not everyone feels amazing all the time. And I certainly don't at the moment.'

'You didn't seem to be feeling unwell last night…'

'Well, you wouldn't have exactly noticed, would you?' she snapped.

'Are you saying you didn't want me? Correct me if I'm wrong, but from what I recall you were a very willing partner—couldn't even wait for me to get out of the shower.'

She flushed a dull red, her body reacting to the image his words evoked, a tide of humiliation burning her up inside. A muscle twitched in his jaw. His face was hard.

'Xavier, it's just desire, purely physical, and, yes…I feel it too. Believe me, if I could switch it off I would.' The ringing bitterness in her tone surprised even her, and she stopped, avoiding his eyes.

He got up with a sudden violent movement, his chair scraping back, loud in the silence of the room. Jane flinched.

'I have business to attend to in the hotel. I'll be back this evening.'

A huge lump grew in her throat and tears blurred her vision as she sat there, miserable after he'd stalked out, unable to take even a sip of coffee. They were no better than bickering children…and it would only get worse. She knew the barbs would get sharper, cut deeper.

She blinked back the tears and hid her face when Yvette

bustled in and clucked like a mother hen. She went up to the bedroom and tried to take a nap, but it was impossible to sleep. She went down and helped make lunch, and prepared for dinner later as it was Yvette and Jean-Paul's night off, but her mind still churned, her stomach feeling acidy. In the afternoon, feeling as though she was going to go out of her mind, she made her escape and fled. She took the car on a drive, not knowing where she was headed.

She found herself arriving at the small cove where they'd spent their last day together in the summer. Grey skies and pounding waves reflected her mood effortlessly. She remembered the sweet happiness she'd felt that day...feelings that had long been submerged by now.

Her thoughts went inward. All along, since they'd met again, Xavier had professed to being motivated by nothing other than wanting this heir. The warmth they had shared in the summer had been the smooth, urbane playboy part of him. The seductive man beneath the cynical, ruthless businessman. She only had to remind herself of how, once he had taken the decision to marry her, he'd gone to New York for two weeks, not to see her again until their wedding day. Supremely confident that she'd acquiesce.

She had thought she was doing the best thing for the baby, for her mother...but all along she had to admit that she had harboured a deep fantasy that maybe things would change, that he would look at her with the same tenderness she remembered from the summer.

She knew it was that that had prompted her to give in to her overwhelming desire...an effort to recapture some elusive dream, maybe change the status quo... But she'd made things worse, not better. And she knew, sadly, even if she could go back to the penthouse suite and that night, she still wouldn't have the strength to watch him walk out through the door. That had been inevitable, a force of nature.

But, because of it, all that stretched ahead for now were

long, lonely days. Nights filled with passion, maybe. But afterwards he would pull away from her, exactly as he had each night up till now, and she would stifle the words that begged for release… She knew it was only a matter of time before she revealed herself, and to do it in a moment of weak passion would annihilate her.

She knew then what she had to do. With a clean, clear certainty in her heart, she felt relieved for the first time in weeks. She would go to him and tell him. She would tell him she loved him, calmly, with dignity, not in a moment of passion.

If there was any way he thought he could feel anything at all beyond a purely physical attraction, then she would stay and try to make the marriage work. But if he couldn't…and that thought made her feel weak…she would leave. As much as it would kill her to do that, it was the only way she could hope to survive.

She could go to the mainland, stay in Lisa's villa, figure out what to do. After all, they were married now, surely the inheritance had to be merely a formality? She wouldn't even insist on a divorce for now, if he didn't want it. But she was sure he would one day…he would meet someone else. How could he not?

Jane got back into the car, a nervous knot in her belly, wanting nothing more than to finally be honest with him…and herself.

By the time she got back to the castle it was much later than she had realized—early evening, the light darkening in the sky. Xavier's Jeep was back already, and Jane felt her stomach plummet. Her hands felt clammy as she gripped the wheel after she'd come to a stop. Could she really go through with this?

Then she saw him at the door, his tall body tense. He strode towards the car, pulling the door open.

'Where the hell have you been?'

Her churning emotions, what she had to do, made Jane

match him in anger. 'I went for a drive. Is that permissible? Don't worry, Xavier, your precious cargo is still safe.'

He frowned down at her as she got out, barely allowing her enough room to move. She clenched her jaw as she brushed against him.

'Cargo…what on earth are you talking about?'

Blue eyes blazing in her face, she looked up after slamming the door shut. 'The baby…the reason we're here.'

His mouth compressed. 'Of course. How could I have forgotten.'

He took her by the elbow and pulled her inside.

'Xavier, let me go. I'm perfectly capable of walking by myself.'

He dropped her arm and rubbed a hand over his eyes. Jane suddenly noticed that he looked terrible, and there was a slight smell of alcohol on his breath.

'Have you been drinking?'

Hard green eyes regarded her as his head came back, nostrils flaring slightly. 'Yes, dear wife. You're driving me to drink…happy now?'

Jane walked towards the kitchen. 'You need a cup of coffee.'

He grabbed her arm and swung her around, bringing her into intimate contact with his whole length. He looked and felt dark and dangerous, dressed all in black. She closed her eyes at the dismayingly predictable way her body responded to his heady proximity. With an effort she held herself stiff as a board in his arms and slowly opened her eyes.

She shook her head at him. 'Xavier, let me go…we can't do this…'

This just firmed her resolve for what she was going to do. Their passion, if unchecked, would soon make them bitter with their need for each other. It was already happening. She pushed herself out of his arms with effort, more from her own self than Xavier holding onto her.

'You're right.' A bleak look crossed his face and he stepped away. 'I'll go and make some coffee. I came home early to talk to you…and then when you weren't here…'

'I…I wanted to talk to you about something too…'

'I'll get us both coffee and bring it into the sitting room.'

He went towards the kitchen and Jane took off her coat, hanging it up and going into the sitting room. She felt ridiculously nervous, pacing up and down, biting her lips, wrapping her arms around her body, sitting down and then standing up.

He appeared at the door silently, with two mugs in his hands. She took the one he handed her. She wrapped her hands around it as if to pull some of the heat into her chilled body. Take some comfort where she could.

She sat on the couch while Xavier stood pensively by the fire.

'Jane, I—'

'Look, Xavier…'

They spoke at the same time. Jane put down her mug and stood up, feeling at a disadvantage sitting down. She locked her hands together to stop the betraying tremor. She needed to calm herself before launching into the hardest confession of her life. She needed time.

She gestured to him. 'You go first…'

He stood for a minute, looking into the fire, before turning towards her. She'd never seen him look so serious, and so distant that it scared her a little. She felt an awful foreboding trickle down her spine.

'Tell me, Jane, does the sight of me really disgust you so much that you can't look at me without your body being rigid with tension?'

'Of course not…how can you say such a thing…?' Her eyes widened in reproach, confusion in their depths, her body going even more rigid despite his words.

'Because ever since we got married you've been like a deer

caught in the headlights…flinching whenever I come near you…rigid like you are now, with that cool icy look in your eyes. Oh, I know how to make you relax—' he laughed harshly '—it's very apparent to both of us how we can make the tension disappear. But then afterwards you can barely wait until I've pulled free of your body before you shut down again.'

Jane blanched at his crude words, remembering all too vividly the night in the penthouse when *he* had been the one to pull away, get out of there as fast as he could. And her humiliation and self-derision rose again like bile.

'It seems to me to be mutual.' She couldn't disguise the bitterness lacing her voice.

He noted it with a look, and emitted an audible sigh. 'I've been thinking all day today about…us. And not just today, if I'm honest. It's something I've tried to avoid thinking about.' He looked into the fire for a moment before looking back at her. 'There's something I should explain, though.'

'Go on.'

She marveled that she sounded so calm.

He thrust his hands into his pockets. 'My parents weren't happily married. By the time my mother died when I was five I was being used as a pawn in their relentless bitter feuds with one another. That's why my father never remarried; he was bitter his whole life, and he took it out on me.' His lips thinned. 'Everyone assumed he never remarried because he loved my mother so much, but it was the opposite. And…I'm afraid that I can see the same thing happening with us. Jane, this morning we were sniping at each other like…exactly how they used to.'

He looked at her, his eyes fixing her with their green luminescence. She took in his words, dimly remembered every time she'd brought up his father, only to have him change the subject, the look that would cross his face. It made sense now. She had to focus when he spoke again.

'I won't bring a child into that again…so that's why I'm

prepared to give you a separation if you want. At least if we're apart, we might be able to maintain respect for each other.'

She stopped breathing. 'What…what do you mean…?' she asked faintly.

'I think we both know this marriage isn't working. You went into this with the clearest of motivations, intentions… and I took advantage of that. The inheritance is assured by our marriage. I shouldn't have brought you back here…'

She couldn't understand how everything wasn't crumbling around her, disintegrating. She sank down onto the couch behind her, her eyes unseeing, unfocused on the ground in front of her.

Xavier's voice continued, like a relentless battering ram against her heart,

'Believe me, I'm tempted to do the cowardly thing, indulge our physical attraction, keep going as if nothing is wrong—and I know you might too, up to a point. I thought it would work…that it would be possible with just…just what we had. But it's not. We're becoming bitter, and that will poison any chance of a civil relationship.'

He was talking about their attraction being the only thing he thought they could have worked on…and even that wasn't enough now.

He paused and took a deep breath. She knew he hated the admission with every bone in his body. It would be hard for him to admit to any frailty, weakness, and their marriage not working would fall under that.

She found herself nodding her head. It was the worst-case scenario. Even knowing that this had happened, *was* happening, she could feel the tiny part of her that had clung to treacherous hope…die.

Just don't make me speak… I can't speak, can't breathe.

'I can set you up wherever you want. If you want to stay

here, I'll go to the mainland. You'll be taken care of... I would just ask that you consider staying in France, so I can have more access to...our child.'

He sounded so cold, so clinical.

She forced herself to stand again, not wanting him to see the devastation on her face, in her body. Well, now she knew. He'd done her the unwitting favour of allowing her to keep her dignity intact. He'd never know how much she loved him.

She looked up, focusing on a point just beyond his shoulder, the lines in her face rigid. He came towards her, she backed away.

'Jane? You can't tell me you're happy...you're not the same person I knew in the summer.'

Neither was he...

'No...I'm not happy.'

That much at least was true.

They faced each other like strangers. A gaping chasm between them.

'You wanted to tell me something?'

She looked at him then, and she had to keep back the slightly hysterical laugh that threatened to bubble out of her mouth. 'Would you believe it was to ask for a separation, too...?'

He sighed heavily. 'Yes, I would. At least it seems we're agreed on this.'

She turned blindly and walked out of the room, just managing to stop herself from running out through the door.

'Jane—wait. We should talk about this now...what we're going to do.'

She turned with huge effort at the door, her face white, her eyes huge blue pools. 'I'm very tired. I'd like to lie down for a while.'

'I'll take the spare room tonight.'

That was all she heard as she walked across the hall, her

singular desire right then to get away to some private space where she could be alone with her pain.

Just as she approached the stairs she had the strangest sensation of not feeling her legs—before a blinding cramp seized her middle and she doubled over in pain. It was so intense that she couldn't breathe. She was vaguely aware of someone calling her name, arms supporting her…and then she collapsed.

She came to for a second, was only half aware of Xavier picking her up into his arms, and then she thought of the baby. Completely forgetting the recent conversation, the uppermost thing in her head with crystal-clear clarity was this baby—and what the future would hold if anything should happen to it

Nothing.

He would send her away, let her go. She clutched his jumper in a white-knuckle grip.

'Xavier…the baby. Nothing can happen to the baby… I need it so much… I love…' And she passed out again.

CHAPTER FOURTEEN

JANE opened her eyes slowly and realised that she was lying on their bed, dim light casting shadows into the room. Then she saw Xavier standing at the base of the bed, talking to some man in a suit. That was weird. Why was she on the bed? And what was that man doing in their room?

She tried to speak and a croak came out. The men turned to face her. The older man hurried to her side. He lifted her hand and took her pulse.

'Hello, my dear, you gave us quite a fright…'

His words meant little to Jane as she struggled to take things in.

'What…what happened?'

She looked from Xavier to the man with a frown on her face.

He sat on the bed and kept her hand in his. 'Jane, I'm Dr Villeneuve. Xavier called me when you collapsed a short time ago. Luckily I was here on the island, doing my rounds, and was close by…otherwise you would have been taken to the hospital on the mainland.'

Suddenly it all came back—every single second of what had happened. Her hand went straight to her belly, her face white.

'The baby…?' But even as she felt her bump, she knew it was all right. The relief she felt made her feel giddy with light-headedness. She caught Xavier's eye, but his face was immobile, shuttered.

Dr Villeneuve patted her hand and looked at Xavier. 'If you'll excuse us for a moment, Xavier? Now that she's awake I'll need to do a thorough exam, just to make sure she's safe to rest here for the night. But she will need to go to the hospital first thing tomorrow.'

'Of course.' Xavier's voice was terse and he left the room.

The doctor helped Jane to undress, and examined her for any signs of anything more serious than a cramp. When she had changed into nightclothes, he came back and sat beside her on the bed.

'Jane…I'm happy enough that nothing is wrong. It's clear that this is stress-related, and it can be common enough, although very frightening. I know it's your first pregnancy, and it can take a lot out of you. You need to take care of yourself…is there anything bothering you?'

She looked into his kind, jovial face and felt like crying.

Only that Xavier doesn't love me and wants to separate…

She shook her head. 'No…don't worry, Doctor. I'll take care of myself and the baby.'

He gestured to the door with a smile. 'And that man out there, wearing a hole in the floor! I've never seen him so frantic. He pulled me out of my car before it had stopped moving. I shudder to think what he would have done if I hadn't been passing. He's asked me to stay for the night, and I'll come to the hospital with you in the morning…he's a very persuasive man.'

She smiled weakly. Xavier's concern for the baby was admirable, but not exactly a soothing balm to her spirit. The doctor left her, and when he was gone she heard his and Xavier's steps echo down the hall.

She sank back into the pillows. The last thing she remembered was Xavier wanting to talk things through, and then that awful pain. She focused on her breathing and staying calm. She wouldn't think about what they had said now…knowing very well that her cramp had been brought on by the sheer shock of Xavier informing her he wanted a separation.

Thank God she hadn't spoken first. To have to separate and have Xavier know how she felt would have made him look at her with such pity…at least this way she could leave, dignity relatively intact.

The door opened and he stood framed in the doorway. Jane's breath stopped, and then quickened as her heart leapt.

'Xavier, the doctor doesn't have to stay. The poor man probably wants to go home to his family.'

'I'm not taking any chances. He's staying, and that's that.'

His tone brooked no argument. He closed the door behind him and came further in, shedding clothes as he did. Jane's mouth went dry as she watched him.

'What are you doing? I thought you said you were going to sleep in the spare room.'

'The doctor is using the spare room.'

'There are at least five more,' she pointed out, an edge of panic strangling her voice.

'And they're all the other end of the house…I won't have the doctor that far away, and you are not sleeping on your own. Anything could happen.'

She averted her face, closing her eyes to his naked body climbing in beside her, her hands clenched under the covers. The doctor had said to stay away from stress—surely this qualified as stress? She could feel her pulse skyrocket.

She lay on her back, eyes closed, and heard the light click off, felt the darkness surround them. Their breathing was unbearably loud to her ears in the quiet room. She could feel a heavy cloud of need and desire hover over them, felt her body coming alive against her will.

Suddenly a gravelly cough from across the hall broke the spell. The doctor. Imperceptibly Jane breathed out a sigh of relief, and turned on her side, willing her body to calm down.

She sank into a deep, dreamless sleep, half waking during

the night to feel herself tucked into Xavier's chest, his head resting on hers, arms tight around her belly and chest, spooning her lower body. In blissful half-consciousness, able to ignore reality, dangerous thoughts, she snuggled in tighter and drifted off again. She told herself this contact was inevitable if they were in the same bed. She knew well enough that morning was just around the corner. And perhaps it was the last time she would ever share a bed with him.

When she woke, sunlight was streaming into the room. Jane took a moment to remember the previous night's events. When she did, a hard weight lodged in her heart. No more hope…no more maybe….no more possibility that perhaps he could come to feel something…

She pulled herself out of the bed, feeling a hundred years old. A small reassuring kick deep in her belly focused her thoughts and reminded her of how close she'd come to nearly losing everything. At least with the baby she'd always have a piece of him.

A movement caught her attention, and she looked up to see Xavier come into the room. He was carrying a tray, and looked smart and cleanshaven, but there were lines around his mouth and circles under his eyes. She willed down the concern that rose up.

'Here's some breakfast. Dr Villeneuve is downstairs, ready to go when you're dressed.'

'I feel much better today. I'm sure I'll be fine. There's no need—'

'Jane. We're going to the hospital.'

He left the tray and walked out. He'd hardly even looked at her.

She forced herself to eat something small, but it tasted like chalk in her mouth. She washed and dressed in jeans and a simple smock top before making her way downstairs.

In no time they were in the chopper, landed, shown to a

waiting car, and then Jane was being settled into a private room at the hospital. The whole thing happened so fast it made her head spin. The nurse left, and then it was just the two of them.

A heavy silence settled over the room. Xavier crossed his arms and rested back against the sill of the window.

'Tell me, I'm interested to know why you were going to ask for a separation…you never did say.'

Her hand stilled on the sheet. The conversational tone he'd used, as if it was as innocuous a comment as asking about the weather, made her see red. The pain and anger she'd been holding in since yesterday evening, the pain that had caused her to cramp, rose like acid bile on her tongue, and she wanted to lash out. Lash out at his cool façade, his reserve, his perfectly articulated reasons why he thought they should separate. As if he was in supreme control, capable of these rational judgements. She wanted to smash through that control…say something to make him squirm…run out through the door and perhaps finally leave her in peace.

She hitched up her chin, looked him in the eye, and with an unwavering voice she was proud of said, 'Would you believe that I was going to ask for a separation because…?' She faltered. Faced with those devastating eyes, her brave façade crumbled, her heart skipped a beat.

'Well…?' he taunted softly, quirking a black brow over cool, sardonic eyes.

It was all the impetus she needed. White hands clenched the bedspread. The full weight of her heartache settled over her like a dark cloud. She felt her voice quaver but didn't care. The words came stumbling, rushing out, tripping over each other…

'Because…Xavier…I love you. I love you so much I can't breathe with it. Every time I look at you I want to make love to you. I hurt all over, but especially in my heart, because you don't love me, and if we don't separate then I'm afraid that by the time this baby is born there won't be anything left of me. Because I just can't bear to be in the same room as you and want you so much, and know that it's only physical attraction you feel, and that you only want me for this baby…' She paused for a second, drawing in a gulping, shuddering breath, too distraught to see how he had straightened and paled. 'And that you don't, can't, *won't* ever love me…that's why…and it's just as good a reason, if not better, than yours.'

Tears blurred her vision and she fought to stop the wobble in her lip, feeling more raw and exposed than she'd ever felt. In shock at what she had just said.

She turned her head away, closing her eyes, the tears trickling down her cheeks as she waited to hear the click of the door. Waited to give in to the huge sobs she could barely hold back, her chest heaving silently.

Instead of the door opening and closing, she felt the bed dip beside her, and a warm hand under her chin, turning her head around. She kept her eyes shut tight, bringing a hand over her face in a pathetic attempt to hide her anguish.

Xavier brought her hand down. The sobs were threatening to break free. She choked them back, opening pain-filled streaming eyes. 'Just go, Xavier…please, leave me alone.'

He was intense, his eyes roving over her face. 'Jane, it's the baby you love, not me.'

How could he do this to her? Humiliate her? Wasn't it enough that she had laid her heart bare for him, and now he had to trample it into the ground? Why wasn't he walking away?

'Xavier, if you can't handle the truth, then leave. This is why I want to separate.'

'But, Jane, all along you've said…' He stopped, started again. 'When you collapsed it was the only thing you mentioned before passing out…'

She pulled his hand down from her chin, saying with a choked voice, 'Of *course* I love the baby…but, like it or not, I love you too. I was scared because this baby is my only link to you. There—are you satisfied? Now, just go and leave me be…*please*.'

He still didn't move. He dropped his head, his hands fists on the bedspread either side of her body. She wiped at the tears on her cheeks and waited for him to stand up and leave, a little hiccup escaping her mouth.

He brought his head up and fixed her with a look of something indefinable that she'd never seen before. Her breath caught in her throat. She couldn't escape his eyes, pinning her to the spot, their brilliant green reminding her of their first meeting.

'Jane…I did think it might be best to separate because of what I told you about my parents. But the stronger reason was that I couldn't live with myself any more for making you so unhappy. Because every time we slept together you were hating me a little more…every time I saw joy in your face for the baby I felt jealous…'

A numbness was taking her over. She recognised it as a form of self-protection. What was he saying?

He went to reach for her hand, but she drew back. He could see the trepidation in her eyes.

'Jane…let me explain. Ever since that night in the penthouse—'

She cut him off, her body taut with tension. 'You were the one who left. And the next morning…you were so cold…'

'I left because…sleeping with you again blew everything out of the water. My feelings didn't go away, they got stronger. And I was jealous…insanely…of your joy in the baby when…when we had just shared…' He stopped himself, a rare vulnerability in his eyes. '*You* were so cool, so blasé about it. As if you'd decided sleeping together was nothing more than giving in to our overwhelming physical urges. I told myself I didn't need feelings to be involved…' He gave a short sharp laugh. 'You were handing me exactly what I thought I wanted, and suddenly it wasn't enough.'

'All *you* want is this baby…'

'I told myself that at the start. I used the baby to justify how much I had to have you, no matter how it happened. When you came to me in London, so self-contained and full of independence, I followed the strongest instinct I've ever felt and did all I could to make you marry me, sure that you'd fall into my bed and we'd pick where we left off and I wouldn't have to examine my feelings.'

'But you— Feelings? You weren't even *thinking* about me…'

'Wasn't I?' He lifted a brow, a rueful look on his face.

Jane still clung onto the protective shield.

'I had your address for two months before I saw you. I had you traced a month after you left… I'll admit I wasn't sure if I was going to get in touch, but I know that I wanted to…and believe me, I didn't like feeling like that.'

She frowned, shaking her head. 'But how…? What about all those women? I saw the papers, all the models…'

He hung his head and groaned before coming back up, his gaze on her mouth, her eyes. 'I took them all out…wined them, dined them…even kissed a few—and as soon as I did the memory of you would break through and any desire I felt disappeared. It happened with infuriating regularity, and no woman…*ever*…has had that effect on me.'

She resisted the pull…dampened the spark that wanted to erupt in her chest.

'But when you asked me to marry you…you left me alone…didn't come back until the wedding.'

'I couldn't be near you. It was too intense. I was terrified of losing you again, and so in denial about how I was feeling that I went as far away as I could…'

He looked away for a moment, then back, a sad light in his eyes. 'After witnessing my parents' fighting, my father's bitterness, I never dared believe I could feel the real thing…I didn't know what it was. This summer you reached a part of me I didn't know existed…then, when you left…'

He looked shamefaced. 'I think on some level I wanted to

tie you to me, sate my desire, which I told myself was the root of all my feelings, and punish you for making me feel so vulnerable. I was so sure you felt nothing for me. But then…it was slowly killing me inside to know how unhappy I was making you. It was the hardest thing I ever did, telling you that you could leave.'

'What…what exactly are you saying?'

She had to be strong. His words still didn't necessarily mean what she thought, hoped. It could just be pity…guilt… and that would kill her all over again.

His eyes stunned her with their intensity. 'Jane, I have not stopped thinking about you since that day you…*we* bumped into each other. It was a *coup de foudre*—love at first sight. I know that now, but it's taken me the longest time to just give in and admit it to myself…'

He grew blurry again through her tears. The spark grew; her heart cracked open.

He tenderly wiped her cheeks with his thumbs, his hands warm around her jaw. She put her hands over his.

'I've been in love with you for so long. I couldn't believe I'd fallen for you that week…' She hiccuped again. 'So stupid.'

'Shh, you don't have to say anything…'

'But I do. I didn't stay in June because I couldn't bear to be just your mistress, especially after Sasha—' She stopped, the pain of that morning still vivid.

Xavier frowned. 'After Sasha, what?'

'She came to the suite that morning and told me that she had organised everything for our date… She told me that it was your usual routine—the pampering, the champagne, dinner…that she did this for all your…women.'

His whole body tensed, his hands dropped. 'No wonder you left… She must have seen that you were different. You have to believe me, Jane. She must have heard me on the phone… I'll bloody kill her.'

He looked so fierce that Jane took his hand. 'I do…I do believe you. I know now that she's no threat.'

She looked down at her hand on his, still not really sure if she could believe. She wanted to tell him…everything.

'When we got married, I didn't sleep with you because I thought you'd guess straight away how I felt. I was so raw and emotional with the pregnancy, and seeing you again…but of course you were right.' She smiled a watery smile, 'What I suppressed only got stronger—the *urges*—God, how I hated using that word—were always there. But using the pregnancy was the only way I knew to try and keep you at a distance. At the ball I wanted to rip the head off every woman there…'

He shook his head ruefully. 'Not sleeping with me was the smartest thing you did…it forced me to face myself. And as for the ball, when I saw you with Pete…he's lucky he got to walk away.'

He looked at her, his face suddenly serious. 'Jane, do you really mean what you said? Are you sure it's not just the baby…?'

'My darling, I loved you long before I found out about the baby…'

He brought his hands up to frame her face again. Jane could feel them tremble. 'When you collapsed in my arms…' He closed his eyes, his skin suddenly ashen. 'If anything had happened to you, I don't think I could have lived. I love you so much that it terrifies me…'

'I'm not going anywhere… I love you, Xavier, with all my heart and soul.'

'And you and this baby—' he bent and pressed a kiss to her belly '—are my heart and soul, *mon coeur*. Without you, my life would be over.'

Then he took her lips in a sweet, healing kiss, a kiss of benediction, and with such reverence that fresh tears streamed down her cheeks—just as the door opened and the doctor walked in.

'What's this? I said no stress.'

They couldn't take their eyes off each other. Jane smiled. 'Everything is just fine.'

Six months later, at the annual summer fête, the island was celebrating. Xavier tucked Jane into his side and held Amelie against his shoulder while she cradled Max against her chest.

Jane's mother and Arthur bustled over. 'You young people need to have fun and relax. We'll take care of the little ones.'

Giving in to a greater force, Jane chuckled as she handed over her son, and watched as Xavier handed over his daughter with comical reluctance and care.

'Will they be OK?' he asked, looking anxiously after the doting elders holding their precious bundles.

Jane slipped her arm around his waist, pushing a hand into one jeans pocket and cheekily squeezing his firm behind. 'Yes, darling, they're taking them for the day—which means I have you all to myself.'

He managed to drag his worried eyes away and brought Jane around to face him, drawing her in tight against his body. She blissfully laced her fingers around the back of his head and moved sinuously against his pelvis, exulting in his low, appreciative groan.

'As I'm not flying in "one of those death traps", as you so succinctly put it—this year or ever again if it reduces you to the terror that you told me it did—then why don't we go somewhere a little more private?'

'Yes, please.'

They walked towards the castle, which wasn't far in the distance, arms wrapped tight around each other.

'Do you think we can find out well in advance if there's any likelihood of twins again? I don't know if I could handle the shock.'

Jane had to laugh out loud as she remembered the moment

that day in the hospital when, during a check-up scan, they had discovered for the first time that she was carrying twins. The doctor had informed them that it was rare, but nevertheless quite possible, for one twin to mask the other until relatively late in the pregnancy.

She pretended to think for a second. 'You know, I must ask Mum. I'm nearly certain there are triplets somewhere on her side...'

He lifted her up into his arms. 'You witch...you just want to see me go into Neanderthal protection mode again...'

'But you did it so well...' She batted her eyelashes up at him.

He claimed her mouth in a hot and desperate kiss. All joking fled from her mind as her pulse speeded up and a familiar throb of desire pulsed through her veins. By the time they got to the front door they were both breathing heavily, with flushed cheeks.

He looked down into her face with such naked love and desire that her heart sang.

'Do you have any idea how happy you've made me?' he asked huskily.

She brought a tender hand up to caress his face. 'If it's half as happy as you make me every day, then we have enough happiness to last a few lifetimes.

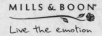

MILLS & BOON®

Live the emotion

0107/01b

Modern
romance™

THE ITALIAN BOSS'S SECRETARY MISTRESS
by Cathy Williams

Rose is in love with her gorgeous boss Gabriel Gessi – but
her resolve to forget him crumbles when he demands they
work closely together…on a Caribbean island! She knows
the sexy Italian is the master of persuasion, and it won't
be long before he's added her to his agenda…

THE KOUVARIS MARRIAGE by Diana Hamilton

Madeleine is devastated to learn that her gorgeous Greek
billionaire husband, Dimitri Kouvaris, only married her
to conceive a child! She begs for divorce, but Dimitri is
determined to keep Maddie at his side – and in his bed
– until she bears the Kouvaris heir…

THE SANTORINI BRIDE by Anne McAllister

Heiress Martha Antonides is stunned when she arrives at
her Greek family home – billionaire Theo Savas has taken
it over! Forced together, they indulge in a hot affair. But
Theo will *never* marry. Although Martha knows she must
leave, her heart and body won't obey her mind…

PREGNANT BY THE MILLIONAIRE
by Carole Mortimer

Hebe Johnson has always secretly admired her wealthy
boss, but she never believed she'd end up sharing his
bed! After one intense and passionate night, Hebe is in
love. But Nick doesn't do commitment… And then Hebe
discovers she's having his baby…

On sale 2nd February 2007

Available at WHSmith, Tesco, ASDA,
and all good bookshops

www.millsandboon.co.uk

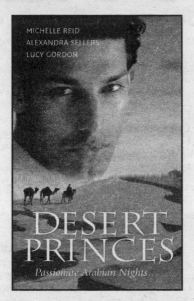

4 FREE

BOOKS AND A SURPRISE GIFT!

We would like to take this opportunity to thank you for reading this Mills & Boon® book by offering you the chance to take FOUR more specially selected titles from the Modern Romance™ series absolutely FREE! We're also making this offer to introduce you to the benefits of the Mills & Boon® Reader Service™—

- ★ FREE home delivery
- ★ FREE gifts and competitions
- ★ FREE monthly Newsletter
- ★ Exclusive Reader Service offers
- ★ Books available before they're in the shops

Accepting these FREE books and gift places you under no obligation to buy, you may cancel at any time, even after receiving your free shipment. Simply complete your details below and return the entire page to the address below. You don't even need a stamp!

YES! Please send me 4 free Modern Romance books and a surprise gift. I understand that unless you hear from me, I will receive 6 superb new titles every month for just £2.80 each, postage and packing free. I am under no obligation to purchase any books and may cancel my subscription at any time. The free books and gift will be mine to keep in any case.

P7ZED

Ms/Mrs/Miss/Mr ....Initials ....
BLOCK CAPITALS PLEASE

Surname ....

Address ....

....

....Postcode................................

Send this whole page to:
UK: FREEPOST CN81, Croydon, CR9 3WZ